THE COMPETITION WAS
HEATING UP

"I've been wanting to do this for some time, Miss Lyford," Lord Harry said, taking Felicity's chin in hand and firmly kissing her.

It was her first kiss, and she was too bemused by the sensation to think of slapping him. Then, suddenly, she was startled to hear Sir Anthony's angry voice, "So, Harry, you force yourself on young girls. It's time to teach you a lesson!"

"No!" said Felicity, hoping to prevent violence. "There was no question of force."

"Are you then so free with your kisses?" Anthony said, and catching her in a powerful embrace, he brought his lips fiercely down on hers.

It was already so terribly hard for Felicity to choose between these two daring and dapper young men—and now it had become even harder. . . .

A
Scandalous Bequest

A Signet Super Regency

"A tender and sensitive love story . . . an exciting blend of romance and history"
—*Romantic Times*

The Guarded Heart

Barbara Hazard

**Passion and danger embraced her—
but one man intoxicated her flesh
with love's irresistable promise . . .**

Beautiful Erica Stone found her husband mysteriously murdered in Vienna and herself alone and helpless in this city of romance . . . until the handsome, cynical Owen Kingsley, Duke of Graves, promised her protection if she would spy for England among the licentious lords of Europe. Aside from the danger and intrigue, Erica found herself wrestling with her passion, for the tantalizingly reserved Duke, when their first achingly tender kiss sparked a desire in her more powerfully exciting than her hesitant heart had ever felt before. . . .

A
Scandalous
Bequest

by
April Kihlstrom

A SIGNET BOOK
NEW AMERICAN LIBRARY

SIGNET TRADEMARK REG. U.S. PAT. OFF. AND FOREIGN COUNTRIES
REGISTERED TRADEMARK—MARCA REGISTRADA
HECHO EN CHICAGO, U.S.A.

SIGNET, SIGNET CLASSIC, MENTOR, ONYX, PLUME, MERIDIAN
and NAL BOOKS are published by NAL PENGUIN INC.,
1633 Broadway, New York, New York 10019

First Printing, September, 1982

4   5   6   7   8   9   10   11   12

PRINTED IN THE UNITED STATES OF AMERICA

I

Miss Felicity Lyford stood at a window overlooking the woods of Lyford Park. This view, however, appeared to afford her little satisfaction. Indeed, Felicity looked as though she had been crying. Behind her, someone stirred and Felicity turned to face her eldest brother. "Why did he do it, Richard?" she asked softly.

"In his blood, I suppose!" he answered roughly. Then, primly, he added, "Not in mine, thank God! Even when Father knew he might lose the estate, he couldn't keep from gambling." Abruptly, Richard Lyford's tone changed as he said, "It's you I'm concerned about, Fay. Father managed to obtain a preferment for me and to purchase colours for John, Neil, and Evelyn, before he went under, but he made no provision for your portion."

Felicity met his eyes steadily as she said, "I know it. Ever since Mama died, Father couldn't bear to look at me. Really look at me, I mean. I can't count the number of times I've had to patch my gowns in the past three years! So it comes as no surprise to me that I am penniless." She paused, fingering the worn

1

wool of her ill-fitting dress, then, taking a deep breath, plunged on, "I've considered the matter carefully, Richard, and I've decided to hire out as a governess."

"*Fay! No!*" the reply came instantly. "A hen-witted notion, if ever there was one! Who is going to hire a girl of less than twenty to be a governess! Especially if there are any sons in the house? You are, though I dislike to say it, devilish good looking, Felicity, and nothing could be more likely to set up a mother's back."

Recognising the deep disapproval in her brother's voice, Felicity barely repressed a grin. *Her* voice, however, was equally serious as she asked, "Very well, Richard, what do *you* suggest I do?"

"Come live with Sally and me," he answered gravely.

Resolutely, Felicity shook her head. "I think not, Richard. Do but consider! Your parish is a good one and I don't doubt you shall be comfortable there, but you don't want me with you. I wouldn't be of much use to you, or to Sally, and should only be in the way."

"I have considered," he answered sternly. "By the provisions of Father's will, *I* am your guardian until you marry and I say you shall come and live with us!"

Felicity had begun to protest such high-handedness, but broke off quickly at the sight of Henshaw, the family butler. Quite properly, Henshaw ignored Felicity and addressed her brother, now the head of the family. "A visitor, sir. A Lady Meecham. I should have denied her admittance, however she says she has come from London."

Richard and Felicity looked at each other in astonishment. "My godmother," she said softly.

"Show her up at once, Henshaw," Richard directed. To Felicity, he said, when they were alone again, "I can not imagine what her purpose is, after all, it is not as though she has shown any great interest in you all these years. Or has she?"

Felicity barely had time to shake her head in denial before Lady Cora Meecham appeared in the doorway of the drawing room. She was a formidable sight, dressed in blue bombazine and an outmoded travelling hat. She leaned on a silver-headed man's cane and surveyed the pair, making no effort to conceal her appraisal. In spite of the shabbiness of the room, and of Felicity's clothes, Lady Meecham seemed to approve. Perhaps it was because Felicity and her brother made such an attractive couple. He was dressed in a sedate blue jacket that had clearly been made by a provincial tailor and his boots lacked the shine demanded by town beaux, but Richard Lyford was a handsome man, particularly when he smiled. He did so now, saying, "Lady Meecham, how do you do? My mother spoke of you often and with much affection. I am Richard Lyford, and this is my sister Felicity."

"Poppycock!" Cora snorted. "Your mama was afraid of me. Nevertheless, I consider it kind of you to say so." She paused to stare at Felicity. In spite of the worn, faded dress that ill-became her, Felicity was a beauty. Or would be, Lady Meecham reflected, if her hair were properly trimmed and arranged and if someone who knew what they were about had the dressing of the girl. Large grey eyes stared out frankly beneath long dark lashes set in a determined face framed by dark curling hair. She would do. Aloud, Lady Meecham said, "You have the look of your mother about you. I was fond of her. Would have come to the funeral, when she died, but your father and I could never abide one another." She paused, seemed to come to a decision, and said, "So now he's dead, too. Why aren't the pair of you in mourning?"

Richard answered for both of them, keeping a tight rein on his temper. "It was my father's express wish that we neither dress in mourning nor withdraw ourselves from society. And though I must strongly deprecate such eccentricity, I feel obliged to follow my father's wishes."

To his astonishment, Cora laughed harshly and sank into a chair as she said, "So he was capable of showing *some* sense, after all! Well, what will you do now? There are four of you, I collect?"

"Five," Richard corrected her politely. "We've three brothers in the military, where they are happy and will continue. I've a living north of here. Felicity, of course, will come and live with me until she marries."

"She will, will she?" Cora asked dryly. "Out with it, girl! What other notions have you been turning over in that quick mind of yours?"

Coming to a decision herself, Felicity straightened her shoulders and answered frankly, "I have been telling my brother, ma'am, that I believe I should prefer to seek a position as a governess or companion or . . . or something. Richard, however, says it won't do. What do you think, ma'am?"

"He's right!" Lady Meecham said promptly. "You're too young and you haven't the fubsy face nor figure for a governess. But," she added, looking at Richard, "I'm not sure your plan is much better, Lyford. I assume you'd like to see your sister married well? Little chance she'll have of meeting eligible young men if she's living in the middle of some obscure village."

Evenly, Richard replied, "No doubt *you* have a suggestion to make?"

"I do. Let me bring her out!" was the astonishing reply.

After a moment of stunned silence, Felicity said, "You must be jesting, ma'am."

"No. Your mother and I had it set between us that I'd bring you out when you came of age to do so. *That* would have been a year ago, but she died and whenever I wrote your father on the matter, he never bothered to reply. Fortunately, he had the good sense to die before you dwindled into a complete spinster. Well? There's nothing to stop you now from coming to London, is there?" that redoubtable lady demanded.

Felicity looked at Richard, who looked back at her helplessly. Finally, taking a deep breath, he said, "The lack of a respectable dowry, or indeed any funds whatsoever, prevents my sister, ma'am. To be honest, we can't afford a Season for Felicity."

Scornfully Lady Meecham retorted, "I'd already guessed as much, Lyford, from her clothes and from the state of Lyford Park as I drove up. Your father never could hold onto money! Should have made it plain what I meant ... I'll frank you, girl."

Richard was first to answer. His face rigidly polite, he said, "How very kind of you, Lady Meecham. I'm afraid, however, that we must decline your very generous offer."

Cora's eyes narrowed as she said dryly, "Oh you must, must you? And how does your sister feel about it? Perhaps I ought to mention that I've a selfish reason behind my offer. I want her to marry my nephew, Sir Anthony Woodhall. Or Lord Harold Eastcott. Either one, it don't much matter."

Slowly Felicity sat down on the window seat. Her voice rather faint and tinged with awe, she said, "Ma'am? Could you explain what you mean? It all sounds rather incredible. How can Sir Anthony *or* Lord Eastcott wish to marry me? So far as I can recall, we've never met!"

Cheerfully Lady Meecham replied, "Oh they don't know they want to marry you. Don't even know you exist. But they will if I bring you out. Perhaps I'd best also mention that I've told my nephews that whichever of the two marries first becomes my sole heir."

Two pairs of eyes stared at her incredulously, then Felicity began to laugh, her sense of the absurd tickled immensely. His cheeks flushed, Richard attempted to ignore his sister as he said stiffly, "I cannot countenance it, Lady Meecham! I am afraid you've gone to a great deal of trouble, coming here, to no purpose. Your scheme is absurd and I couldn't possibly allow Felicity to go with you. Since you have been frank with us, ma'am, I shall be equally frank with you! Do you actually expect my sister to pledge herself to become betrothed to a man she has never met? Is she to set herself to somehow attach the affections of one . . . or both! . . . of your nephews? Particularly *such* nephews? Even so far removed from London as we find ourselves, the reputations of libertines penetrate!"

Angrily, Lady Meecham thumped her cane against the bare floor. "Good God, Lyford! You're almost as big a fool as your father was. And if you wish to speak of libertines——"

"I don't!" Richard retorted, cutting her short ruthlessly. "That is precisely the reason I don't wish my sister to marry one. Though my father's failing was only with cards, not women, I think."

"True," Cora conceded, a trifle more subdued. "Nevertheless, I wish *you* will listen to me, Lyford. And I wish *you*, my girl, would stop laughing!" Felicity hastily apologised and Lady Meecham went on, scarcely mollified, "I'm not asking your sister to pledge herself to marry either one, Lyford. My hope is merely that once they have met her, one of my nephews will form an attachment for Felicity. I am not such a nodcock, however, as to suppose that such an attachment is inevitable! Do consider, Lyford. At the very least, your sister will have a chance to go about in society and may very well form some other eligible attachment, should my hopes prove fruitless. In any event, I pledge to provide Felicity with some portion. I only ask, girl, that you not be so missish as to spurn my nephews out of hand! Come, Miss Lyford! Your brother has been plain with me, I ask you to do the same. Are you as prudish as Lyford? Do my nephews' reputations preclude them as possible husbands for you?"

Felicity no longer had any desire to laugh. It was several moments before she answered, but when she did, her voice was soft and steady. "No, they do not. I *shall* be frank, however, Lady Meecham, and say that your scheme seems absurd to me also. But that is your affair. If you truly mean that I need not accept Sir Anthony or Lord Eastcott unless an attachment is formed, then I would indeed accept your generous offer."

Both Lady Meecham and Richard spoke at once. "Good girl!"

"Felicity, are you mad? I won't allow it!"

Felicity chose to answer her brother first. She sounded close to tears as she said, "Why not, Richard? It is, I confess, a scheme I cannot altogether like, but what choice have I? You say I cannot be a governess. Very well, what alternative is left me? I love you and Sally dearly, but the notion of dwindling into a lonely old maid in a Yorkshire parish frightens me! I'm young and would like, for once in my life, to know a little fun. Do you know that I've never yet danced until dawn or been sent flowers or been away from home except to go to school for *one year*? Can you even imagine what my life has been like since Mama died? I tell you I *will* go to London, Richard."

"If you had only written to me," Lyford tried to expostulate.

"Written?" she asked bitterly. "And what would that have accomplished? Everyone said my place was here, with Father. And if he would not listen to *our* curate's protests at his neglect of me, why should he have listened to yours?" Felicity paused and shook her head. "I blame none of you, Richard, but it is the outside of enough for you to tell me you won't allow the one chance I have of a Season . . . of some pleasure!"

Stunned by this unexpected outburst from a sister he thought he knew well, Richard Lyford tried to make amends. "Felicity, if you really wish to go to London, then go. I shan't forbid it."

With a wry smile, Felicity thanked him. She then turned to Lady Meecham, who appeared to have been watching this exchange with something akin to delight. "When do you wish me to come to London?" Felicity asked quietly.

Lady Meecham answered swiftly, "At once! Today. There's nothing to keep you any longer, is there? Lyford Park goes on the auction block tomorrow to meet your father's debts and I cannot believe you would wish to remain for that. And since old Lyford declared you wasn't to go into mourning, I may as well bring you out as soon as possible."

Reminded of *that* grievance, Richard said irritably, "I am not at all sure we should obey him in the matter. You may approve, ma'am, but will the rest of society?"

"With me to back Felicity, they will!" Lady Meecham replied firmly. "Nor will anyone be very surprised, considering your father's reputation as an odd 'un."

"Perhaps, Lady Meecham," Felicity said in a quiet well-bred voice, "we'd best clarify one matter. If I am to come and stay with you for the Season, I must tell you that I will not tolerate criticism of my father."

The old woman thumped her cane but nodded approvingly. "Good! You don't want for spirit, which is as well since I can't abide milk-and-water misses. Well, when can you be ready to go?"

"Within the hour," was Felicity's instant reply. "I haven't much to pack, you see. I assume I am to bring my abigail, as well?"

"Of course. We shan't make the mistake of offending convention more than need be. And, in any case, you'll want someone you know about you to help you dress and so on." Lady Meecham hesitated, smiled, and said, "You won't find me a nipcheese, I promise you!"

The Lyfords were generally sturdy looking people, but Felicity was built on more delicate lines and she almost gave the impression of being like a bit of thistledown as she left the room. His face still stern, Richard asked Lady Meecham if she cared for any refreshments while she waited. Cora waved away the question and instead said bluntly, "Still don't approve, do you, Lyford?"

"My sister has made her choice."

"Aye, and a sensible choice, though you can't see it! True, I'm an old woman with an odd fancy, but I keep my promises. My nephews know that, if you don't! Your sister will have her Season and, if she keeps her wits about her, a husband at the end of it. Even if it's not one of my nephews." She paused, then sighed. "Never mind. Talking won't convince you. Bring me some sherry, if you have any, and perhaps a few biscuits to tide me over."

Richard bowed, evidently relieved to be spared any further catechism. "I'll see to it at once, if you'll excuse me. I'd ring for it but I prefer not to ask the servants to climb the stairs twice . . . particularly as I can barely pay their wages now. My father, of course, made no provision for them in his will."

"Well, go along and don't worry about leaving me alone, I shan't mind," Lady Meecham said generously. Then, shrewdly, she added, "No doubt you also intend to argue with your sister, but I think you'll find she knows her own mind."

Richard bowed again, acknowledging the hit, and left the room. Lady Meecham leaned back in her

chair, a satisfied smile on her lined face. Perhaps she
was a fool, but by God she would enjoy this Season!
Anthony would be appalled, of course, if he knew
what she was about, but it was high time he and his
cousin settled down. And not with any of those bits of
muslin Anthony was so fond of. Though if he'd kept
to those bits of muslin, Cora might not have felt
pressed to take action just yet. It was his dangling after the Carrington chit that worried Lady Meecham.
The girl was a beauty but heartless, and so Cora had
told her nephew bluntly. His only response had been
to laugh harshly and say, "Then we are well matched,
ma'am, for so, too, am I heartless."

It was then that Cora had made up her mind to do
something. As she had told Lyford, she would have
offered, in any case, to present Felicity. But it was
desperation that had led her to concoct this scheme.
Well, she was an old woman with the money to indulge her whims, so why not? And if that scheme
failed? Why then there was Harold. Lady Meecham
could not suppress a certain amount of anxiety over
his activities either. If Sir Anthony and Miss Lyford
chose not to make a match of it, Cora would be satisfied if Harold wed the girl and settled down. She was
quite out of the common way and with far more spirit
than her brother. With Cora to prod them along,
surely one of her nephews would throw the glove to
Felicity? Thinking of Richard, Lady Meecham was
amused. What, she wondered, was the young ass saying to his sister?

Whatever it was, it didn't signify for Felicity Lyford and her abigail were ready sooner than Lady
Meecham expected. Miss Lyford was pale but calm,
dressed warmly for the drive in clothes that had obvi-

ously been handed down from her mother. The
abigail looked excited and disapproving at the same
time. She was an older woman who treated Felicity
with the familiarity of a family retainer. Richard
stood beside them as Henshaw helped Lady
Meecham with her cloak. "Ready?" she snapped at
Felicity.

The girl met her eyes steadily. "Quite ready,
ma'am."

"Then let's be off. I've no fancy to be caught in a
snowstorm," Cora said, starting for the carriage.

Lyford followed, directing the placement of Felicity's small amount of baggage. Then he prepared to
hand her into the coach after Lady Meecham.
"Good-bye, Fay. Remember! Any time you wish, Sally
and I shall be happy to welcome you to come live
with us!"

Felicity looked up at his stern face, her eyes dancing. "I do know it, Richard! But confess! I should be a
sad trial to you there, languishing away when I might
be dancing in London."

"Just remember!" he repeated stubbornly. Then, a
smile tugging at his own face, he added, "And do try
to curb your levity, Felicity. Otherwise I fear you will
find yourself in the basket."

"Why then you will have your wish and I shall
have to come back to you," she teased him gaily.

Richard only shook his head at her, however, then
turned to her maid and said, "Take care of her, Annie."

"I shall, sir. As much as she'll let me!"

A few moments later, the door was shut and Lyford
stepped back. The antiquated coach pulled away
from the house and down the drive toward the gates

of Lyford Park. For a long time Richard just stood there, looking after them, and the first few flakes of snow began to fall. Concerned, Henshaw joined his master on the steps and said, "Sir? Shouldn't you come in? Don't want to catch cold, do you?"

Startled at this intrusion upon his thoughts, Richard looked at the butler. "Yes, Henshaw, you're quite right. Let's go in. It won't be the same, though, without little Felicity."

"No, sir. Begging your pardon, but it won't be. Mrs. Henshaw is fond of saying that Miss Felicity brightened up the place. P'rhaps it's just as well the place is to be sold, seeing as how all the Lyfords are gone away. And even these past few years Mrs. H and I have felt the place hasn't been kept up as it ought to be. Begging your pardon, sir, if I've been speaking too freely."

Richard smiled at the fellow. "No, how could you offend, Henshaw, when I know very well it's been more than six months since my father paid your wages. I only hope the new owner of Lyford Park will value you as you're worth, for God knows I haven't the money to provide for you as my father should have done!"

"Ah, well, Mrs. Henshaw and I, our needs haven't been so great. And we're young, yet. We'll manage. So will the others. It's Miss Felicity we've been worrying about. Begging your pardon, sir, but we all know as how you and your brothers have been provided for, but not her. Having seen her grow up, as you might say, we worry about her, we do."

"So do I, Henshaw, so do I. She's on her way to London and now we must trust to God—and Lady

Meecham—to watch over her. Perhaps she'll find a husband there."

"I hope so sir." Then, straightening, Henshaw said more briskly, "Well, I'd best go down to the kitchens, sir. What with Mrs. H crying and all, we're not likely to have any supper, else! But do come in now, sir."

"I shall, Henshaw, I shall."

II

As Lady Meecham's travelling coach conveyed its mistress and her young guest back to London, three gentlemen stood together in the library of Sir Anthony Woodhall's townhouse. One of them was George Aylesbury, and he quickly retreated to the relative quiet of a far corner of the room, correctly assuming that Sir Anthony's other guest had no desire to speak to him. Sir Anthony, meanwhile, stood with his back to the crackling fireplace and surveyed his very elegant cousin, Lord Harold Eastcott. "Well, Harry?" he asked briskly. "I've postponed my drive in the park for you and I trust the matter at hand is truly urgent?"

Forced to look up at his cousin, Lord Eastcott perceived that he had made a tactical error in so quickly seating himself. It was therefore with a trace of impatience that he retorted, "Damme, cousin, you must know why I've come! Aunt Cora's man of business must have called on you as he did me?" Harry paused and Sir Anthony briefly inclined his head. "Well, then?" Harry demanded. "Don't tell me you're pleased? The old lady must be daft!"

"Have you, er, expressed that view to our Aunt Cora?" Sir Anthony asked with some amusement.

For a moment, Lord Eastcott forgot to drawl. "No, I didn't. She's not at home."

"My sympathies," Sir Anthony said politely.

"Damme, Tony, don't play off your airs at me! What the devil are we to do about this?" Eastcott demanded.

"Why do anything?" Anthony retorted. "I thought the matter tolerably clear. Either we marry or we don't. As for me, I intend to ignore the matter. I refuse to allow myself to be dictated to."

Lord Harry eyed his cousin with gloomy disfavour though not even the celebrated Beau Brummell could have found anything to cavil at in Sir Anthony's appearance. Woodhall wore a coat of blue superfine whose fit bespoke Weston. A snowy cravat was arranged in the intricate style called the Oriental, while fawn breeches and gleaming hessians proclaimed Sir Anthony to be a man of fashion. Moreover, dark eyes and neatly cropped dark hair topped a tall, deceptively slender frame that women were inclined to admire. Finally, Harry drawled, a trace of venom in his voice, "Oh, of course *you've* no need to regard Aunt Cora's nonsense. How could I forget how well breeched you are?"

Sir Anthony gave a shout of laughter. "Lord, Harry! Surely you cannot fault me for that? Rather blame your father."

Lord Eastcott found himself silenced, but only for a moment. "Let us speak plainly, cousin. You know I need more blunt."

"To pay your tailor, no doubt."

Lord Eastcott scowled at this reference to his exces-

sively elegant appearance. Normally, Harry felt quite
proud of the way he looked. A tall, well-built man,
dressed in the first stare of fashion, he ought to have
outshone his cousin. The fact was, he did not. Perhaps
it was the lines beginning to appear in his fair face, or
the faint hint of arrogance that clung to Lord Eastcott, but whatever the reason, he showed to disad-
vantage beside Sir Anthony.

Evidently deciding that his cousin would not answer unprompted, Sir Anthony said abruptly, "I fail
to see how *your* need for money concerns *me*. If you
choose to marry at once, to meet the terms of Aunt
Cora's will, surely I have nothing to say in the matter?"

Lord Eastcott continued to regard his cousin with
disfavour. "Come, come, Tony. I have always regarded your understanding as quite superior. Are
your intentions toward Miss Lucinda Carrington serious?" At the sound of the young woman's name, Sir
Anthony ceased to lounge against the wall and instead drew himself erect, frowning. As Eastcott went
on, the frown deepened. "Are your feelings attached,
Tony? Or would you consider relinquishing your pretensions? You could quite easily do so, if you chose."

"But I don't choose, my dear Harry," Sir Anthony
drawled in a voice that matched his cousin's. Woodhall smiled lazily now, but the smile did not reach his
eyes. "Nor do I intend to delay any wedding plans
merely to oblige you. Not," he added with a genuine
smile at Harry's expression of horror, "that I have any
such plans at the moment."

Forcing himself to lean back and relax, Harry
negligently crossed one leg over the other and
brought his fingertips together. "I have often won-

dered," he said, "why you should be so attracted to Lucinda. One would have thought she was not quite in your style."

"I collect you would say she is *your* style?" Woodhall asked, a glint in his eye.

Eastcott shrugged. "More so than yours. We understand each other."

"Yet I had not guessed an announcement was imminent," Sir Anthony said pointedly.

Now Lord Harry smiled and waved a hand airily. "Oh, as to that, without Aunt Cora's will there would naturally have been no question of my marriage to Miss Carrington. One must, after all, be practical, and Miss Carrington's portion can be no more than genteel."

"In short, quite insufficient for your purposes?" Sir Anthony hazarded.

"Quite!' Harry agreed with the same lazy smile. "And, in any event, Miss Carrington is not precisely unambitious herself. Aunt Cora's will, however, alters everything."

"Forgive me," Woodhall said politely, "but I am surprised you do not seek a less risky target. I might, after all, precede you in matrimony even were I to relinquish my pretensions, as you call them, to Miss Carrington's hand. You might then lose all."

Lord Eastcott sent his cousin a withering look. "My dear Tony, you need not spare my feelings! You know as well as I that few mothers will open their doors to me, and none with heiresses in their care."

The smile vanished from Sir Anthony's face as he replied coldly, "Once more I must point out that that is none of my affair."

Eastcott shrugged angrily. "Yes, well, how was I to know the chit would spread the tale?"

"There ought to have been no tale to spread," Woodhall retorted coldly. "In any case, something must have been suspected when you pinked her father in a duel. Surely it consoles you that the young lady was more thoroughly ruined by the elopement even than you?"

"You wrong me!" Harry answered, no longer the dandy. "I would not have seen her hurt for the world. It was, you know, marriage I intended."

Woodhall sighed. "And you were but eighteen yourself. I know, cousin. The world, however, is less understanding than I."

For a brief moment there was a trace of the old friendship between them. Then Anthony asked quietly, "Did you have to set out to prove to the world that its opinion of you was justified?"

Eastcott shrugged and he was, once more, the dandy. "Ah, but my nature, Tony! I could not resist, you see, testing just how much my fellow men would believe of me. And, in time, I discovered depravity to be be so much more fascinating than virtue."

Sir Anthony favoured his cousin with a bow as he said, "In that event, Harry, you have made your choice and ought to be willing to abide the consequences."

"But I am not willing!" Eastcott retorted with amusement. "One of the advantages of being a scoundrel is that one need not be reasonable. Besides, what have I to lose? Come, come, Tony! At least be honest enough to admit that you envy my freedom. And don't, I pray you, point out that I am so free I must needs dance to the tune of my aunt's will."

Sir Anthony laughed and said, with one of his rare smiles, "If I envy you at all, Harry, it is for your ease with the ladies. The mamas may be able to resist your charm, but you've success enough with most."

"Mamas and heiresses," Lord Eastcott amended with a sigh. It was to be noted, however, that there was a distinct twinkle to his eyes as he added, "I have often thought, Tony, that had I *your* fortune, or you *my* address, no lady's heart would be safe."

"You forgot to add your tailor," Sir Anthony shot back. "While I may always be accounted *properly* dressed, it is you who are noted for a certain flair."

This time Lord Eastcott did not object to the reference to his appearance. His good humour restored, he was at his best and he knew it. So now Harry grinned and said, "It is, I assure you, the sole reason I have not been clapped up in Newgate. I never pay my tailor, but he has long since ceased to dun me, having decided that I am such a credit to his establishment that the satisfaction of sending me to gaol would be far outweighed by the loss of such an excellent advertisement of his skill." He paused and held out his well-shod foot. Surveying it regretfully, Eastcott said, "My bootmaker, on the other hand, is not so perceptive."

Sir Anthony laughed, then shot his cousin a keen glance. "Is it serious this time?"

Lord Eastcott shrugged impatiently. "It is always serious, cousin. Were I not so lucky at Ascot and at the gaming tables, I must have been rolled up long ago. But with luck I'll come about. In any event, the news of Aunt Cora's will shall buy me time."

Sir Anthony stiffened. "Do you mean to say, Harry, that you *expect* the news to get about?"

Lazily, Harry rose to his feet, topping Sir Anthony's tall frame by an inch. With amusement he drawled, "But of course, Tony. If Aunt Cora does not set it about, I shall. Surely you must see that the gossip can only help me? Why, the fair Lucinda herself must needs become aware of it, else I should have no chance whatsoever of beating you to the altar. Now don't, I pray you, waste your energy on useless anger," he counselled his cousin. "Spend it instead contemplating how you shall face the gossip. And with that advice, Tony, I bid you good day!"

With a careless wave of his hand, Lord Eastcott ambled toward the door, retrieving his cane as he did so. Sir Anthony's ire could not last long and he was able to call out to his cousin, "And I bid you good fortune, Harry!"

As the outer door closed behind Eastcott, Sir Anthony turned to find his friend Aylesbury contemplating him. "I hope you will forgive me, Tony, if I say that I do not find your cousin as amusing as you seem to," Aylesbury said as he set the book he was holding back on the shelf.

"Nevertheless, he is my cousin," Sir Anthony pointed out gently, "and if he is rather wild, the fault must lie at least partly at my aunt—his mother's—door. I reveal no secrets if I say he is but following in her footsteps."

Aylesbury snorted. "It's common knowledge, to be sure, that Lady Eastcott was accustomed to flaunt her affairs abroad and, moreover, involve young Harry in most unpleasant scenes. But the devil take it, Tony, I still cannot like what I see in him—whatever the cause!"

Sir Anthony nodded heavily. "Nor I. But I recall,

you see, the young boy my own age who hunted and fished and wrestled with me at my father's estate, whenever matters grew too unpleasant at his own."

Aylesbury shot a shrewd glance at his friend. "Company for you, wasn't he? With two sisters and no brothers you'd likely have been glad of that. Particularly——"

He was cut off by the appearance of a servant. "Your mother, Sir Anthony, requests your presence," the fellow announced impassively.

Aylesbury and Woodhall exchanged glances, then Sir Anthony said quietly, "Thank you, Thomas. I shall be there directly. You will excuse me, George, I know."

"Of course."

Sir Anthony smiled. "Mind you, I shall expect you to wait. I've not forgotten our wager!"

His friend laughed and, taking a seat, retorted, "Nor I! I've no intention of leaving until we settle the matter!"

Grinning, Woodhall followed the footman from the room. He was not smiling, however, when he entered his mother's sitting room. "You sent for me, ma'am?"

For a moment, Lady Woodhall merely regarded her offspring sadly. She made a lovely picture, delicate and interestingly pale as she reclined on a chaise longue wearing an exquisite dressing gown of seafoam green embroidered in silver thread, a lace cap over her blond curls. Lady Woodhall was as fair as her son was dark and had, in her day, been acclaimed a beauty. Even now she looked more than a decade younger than her years. Unfortunately, a once gentle disposition had been strained and turned shrewish by the several very real illnesses that had left Lady

Woodhall generally an invalid. It was therefore a snappish voice that answered, "Had you the courtesy to visit me more often, Anthony, I would not need to send for you! What the servants must think of this I—"

"Let us concede, ma'am, that I lack proper filial respect," he said wearily, "and discuss, instead, whatever is on your mind."

Without looking at the woman, Lady Woodhall dismissed her companion. "You may leave us, Maria."

Impassively, Sir Anthony held the door open for the nondescript woman who nervously edged past him. When the door was once more shut, Lady Woodhall demanded, "Is it true? Has my sister actually written such an improper will?"

In spite of himself, Sir Anthony was amused. "Now how do you know? Has she written to tell you so also, Mama?"

Lady Woodhall leaned further back against the cushions. "So it's true. Cora always was a madcap, but this goes beyond the line, and so I shall tell her! I do not know how to bear it. Depend upon it, the news will somehow get about and the entire ton will be laughing at us!"

"Well, yes," Sir Anthony said apologetically, "you are correct. The news *will* get about. Harry informs me that it is in his interest to see that it does so."

"*Harry!*" Lady Woodhall shuddered. "I have never understood what my brother was about, marrying Theresa! And her son is just like her. And your father used to encourage that woman. In fact—but I will not speak of *that!*"

Sir Anthony's lips were pressed into a thin angry line as he said, "Just as well, ma'am. My father was a kind man with an ear for anyone who was troubled and needed a shoulder to lean on."

"Kind?" Lady Woodhall laughed harshly. "Oh, aye, kind! Particularly to my sex! And, as you so helpfully point out, totally without discrimination. *You*, I know, disbelieve me. But let me tell you that your father never bothered to deny it."

"Perhaps he felt no need," Sir Anthony snapped. Then, recollecting his father's face, he went on more gently, "Perhaps he felt you had the need to vent your spleen at him, ma'am. He loved you deeply, you know, even if you cannot believe it."

Lady Woodhall turned her face away, silent for a moment. When she did speak, it was in an altogether different voice, a gentler voice. "On that head, let us speak no more! I can only wish it were true. Tell me instead, Anthony, what you intend to do about Cora's will."

"Do? Why nothing," he shrugged.

Lady Woodhall hesitated, then probed, "I have heard your attentions toward Miss Carrington grow particular?"

For once, Sir Anthony took no offence. "It is, I believe, time to consider marriage, ma'am. Miss Carrington is of respectable lineage and her disposition . . . even."

"Even? I should rather have termed it cold!" Lady Woodhall retorted. "And if she is like her mother. . . . But never mind that. Is she not rather . . . *old?*"

"Twenty-three," he answered woodenly. "In short, old enough, and by temperament well-bred enough, not to enact me any Cheltenham tragedies."

"As I suppose you'll say I did to your father?" She

sniffed. Her ladyship distinctly sniffed. "Oh, Anthony, I have often wished our lives had gone differently!"

Her words ended on a wail and Sir Anthony swiftly crossed the room to his mother's side. "I assure you, Mama, that my father understood and did not hold it against you. And if I . . . if I cannot be so understanding, forgive me. But since I cannot, I think it best I choose someone like Miss Carrington."

Lady Woodhall shook her head and sighed. "How I wish, Anthony, you could have known us when Woodhall and I were young and in love. Before I was ill. You would not then speak so coldly of marriage. Believe me, those brief years of happiness were worth all the rest!"

Sir Anthony smiled at his mother but answered ruefully, "Unfortunately, ma'am, I did not and, in any case, must make my own choice for myself."

Lady Woodhall nodded and sighed yet again. Then, shaking herself, Lady Woodhall forced herself to speak lightly. "Well, I shan't scold at you any longer. No, nor hold you at my side, for I am persuaded you must have all manner of appointments waiting on you. Go and enjoy yourself, my dear. Just remember to visit me now and then, will you?"

"I shall," he assured her.

Sir Anthony kissed his mother's hand as a parting salute, then hastily made good his escape, seeking out his friend Aylesbury who, true to his word, was still waiting in the library. Aylesbury looked up from the book he was reading and favoured his friend with a sympathetic look. "Devil of a humour, was she?" he asked. Sir Anthony's only response was to stare quellingly at his friend, who sighed and said ruefully, "I

know—my deplorable want of tact! Well, don't eat
me, Tony. Shall I apologise?"

Sir Anthony shook his head at Aylesbury, knowing
that his blunt friend meant well. Short and stocky,
dressed to please himself rather than the dictates of
fashion, with a countenance *not* inclined to please the
ladies, Aylesbury nevertheless was granted the entrée
everywhere and genuinely welcomed. It was impossible to be angry with the fellow! It was Woodhall's
turn to sound rueful as he answered, "No, you need
not, George. You do know, though, it's only her poor
health that makes her so . . . puts her so out of countenance? We, too, should find ourselves less than amiable were *we* cooped up all day!"

For a moment, Sir Anthony stood lost in his own
thoughts and Aylesbury made no attempt to rouse
him. Then, as if consciously trying to throw off his
foul mood, Woodhall said briskly, "Come, George!
We still have that wager to settle! Let us go for that
drive and see if these greys are not the sweet-goers I
promised you."

Aylesbury nodded and closed the book he held
with a clap and set it down. Then, as he stood, he
said cheerfully, "Indeed. And p'rhaps we'll even encounter the enchanting Miss C!"

Sir Anthony smiled and shook his head, but Aylesbury was soon proved correct. In spite of all the
delay, it was still the fashionable hour to ride, drive,
or promenade in the park when Woodhall's curricle
reached the gates. And Miss Lucinda Carrington was
not one to eschew such a promising opportunity to
encounter her many admirers. When Sir Anthony es-
pied it, Lucinda's carriage was surrounded by young
men. She looked enchanting in a warm pelisse of

deep blue trimmed with fur and a matching bonnet over her guinea-gold curls. As Woodhall's curricle approached, Lucinda smiled invitingly and commanded her admirers to make way for Sir Anthony and his friend. When he had pulled up abreast of her, Lucinda chided playfully, "Why, Sir Anthony, I almost begin to think you a stranger! Surely it has been four days since I have seen you?"

As he returned a light answer, Woodhall could not help wondering if Harry was right. Would Miss Carrington favour himself and Eastcott more once she learned the terms of Cora's new will? And would it matter to him if she did? He even wondered, for a brief moment, if he shouldn't simply resign himself to bachelorhood. Lucinda, ever alert to the mood of an admirer, was not pleased by Woodhall's air of abstraction, but she was too clever to chide him for it. Instead she said lightly, "You'd best look to your horses, Sir Anthony! I vow the gentleman who wishes to pass is developing a temper!"

Hastily, Sir Anthony looked around and spied the angry fellow whose carriage he did indeed block. With a smile for Lucinda he said, "Then I'd best be off. Good day, Miss Carrington!"

"Good day, Sir Anthony," she replied demurely.

As they pulled away, Aylesbury observed, "I suspect all of London will heave a sigh of regret when the fair Lucinda weds."

"Yes, if you discount the ladies!" Woodhall cheerfully retorted. "And you. Don't try to gammon me into believing you form one of her court! Indeed, I should almost say you hold her in dislike."

"I?" Aylesbury asked. "I should never be so uncivil. Let us merely say that I am so wanting in taste as to be unable to appreciate Miss Carrington's charms. I am sure it is deplorable and indicates poor blood somewhere in my background, but there it is! I believe I should much prefer to marry a girl with warmer blood in her veins. And no doubt it's absurd of me, but I rather believe in love."

Woodhall was silent a moment, then he said quietly, "Do you know, George? I almost think I envy you."

III

Once again Felicity Lyford stood at a window looking out, but this time the view was of a London street and it was raining outside. Just as the view had changed, so too was Miss Lyford different—at least in appearance. Her hair curled about her head in a soft cap, making her look younger than her nineteen years. Her dress was of sprigged muslin and was as impractical, on such a chilly day, as it was elegant and fashionable. Fortunately for Felicity's comfort, a generous fire was burning in the grate for, as Lady Meecham had said, there was nothing nipcheese about *her*. Indeed, everything about the tastefully furnished silver and blue drawing room bespoke a preference for elegance over economy. All these circumstances combined to give Felicity a poise she had never had before and that even the dismal day could not dispel.

Just as Felicity was wondering when Lady Meecham would return from a morning call, the door of the drawing room opened and Tifton announced, "Sir Anthony Woodhall."

Startled, Felicity nevertheless managed to say, "Show him up."

It was unconventional, to be sure, for her to see any young man alone, but Felicity could not see how to rebuff her benefactress's nephew. Particularly as Felicity was certain Lady Meecham would not wish her to do so. Unprepared as she was, however, to meet Sir Anthony so soon, Felicity was hard-pressed to greet him calmly. He entered the room quietly and stopped just over the threshold to look at her. Conscious of her rising colour, Felicity stammered, "Hello, sir. I . . . I am sorry but Lady Meecham is out, at present. If . . . if you would care to wait, I expect her to return soon. I am Felicity Lyford and I . . . I am residing with Lady Meecham for the Season."

His eyes raked her from head to foot and his lips seemed to curve in distaste as Woodhall replied curtly, "Yes, well, I have come not to see my aunt, Miss Lyford. I have come to see you."

Felicity returned Woodhall's stare with frank astonishment. With difficulty, she forced herself to ignore the hostility in his voice and say, "Perhaps you will be good enough to explain what you mean, sir? Pray be seated."

"Thank you, but I prefer to stand!" he retorted coldly.

Her temper beginning to be aroused, Felicity answered, "Well I prefer to be seated!" She crossed the room, sat in a comfortable chair by the fire, and then added, "I am waiting for your explanation, sir."

Felicity was forced to wait several minutes more before Woodhall deigned to speak. She chose to use the time to study Sir Anthony as openly as he had appraised her. He was, she noted, quite as tall as her

brother Richard, with a deceptively slender build.
Deceptive because it gave no hint of the strong
muscles Felicity felt sure he possessed. His dark hair
was carefully dishevelled, and his boots gleamed in a
way that Felicity's brothers' boots never had. An im-
peccably tailored coat topped fashionably yellow pan-
taloons, while his intricately tied neckcloth argued an
expert's touch. Indeed, the overall neatness of his person argued a deep concern for, and pride in, his appearance. Had his face not been so forbidding,
Felicity would have had no trouble understanding
why, at twenty-seven, he was a most sought-after
young man.

His countenance, however, *was* forbidding. As he
looked at Felicity, Sir Anthony saw a fashionable
young woman with disconcertingly large eyes. Far
from affording him satisfaction, however, these observations only caused Woodhall to press his lips more
tightly together. So the girl wished to know why he
was here, did she? Well he would be happy to tell
her! "I have come, Miss Lyford, to see if the reports
about you are true," he said arrogantly.

"And are they?" she disconcerted him by replying.

Nettled, Sir Anthony retorted, "Very much so. You
are as lovely as I was told, and as cold. I have little
trouble believing that you are, indeed, plucking my
aunt of her fortune."

With a gasp, Felicity was on her feet, white with
fury. "Is that truly what is being said about me?"

"By the family lawyers, yes!" Sir Anthony answered
promptly. He paused to note with satisfaction her
now flushed face, then pressed on harshly, "Can you
deny that my aunt has been spending large sums on

you? For dresses and God knows what else? Or that she has agreed to dower you?"

"How many people know of this?" Felicity whispered, shaken.

"Very few!" was the sardonic reply. "You cannot think that I would wish the entire ton to know of my aunt's folly. She and I share the same man of business, however, and he felt it his duty to warn me of the harpy who has attached herself to my aunt!"

Rage carried Felicity beyond prudence and she said, "Oh, yes, now I recollect. You, Sir Anthony, are likely to be her principal heir and cannot bear the notion of your aunt squandering her fortune on her own pleasure instead of saving it for you!"

Furious, Sir Anthony advanced menacingly until he towered over Felicity and it almost seemed he would shake her. But he did not. Instead he said coldly, "I have no objection to my aunt spending her money on *herself.*"

"How fortunate, Tony, since you've nothing to say in the matter!" came a languid voice from behind them.

"Harry!" Woodhall said, in a voice that held no welcome.

Lord Eastcott ignored his cousin and spoke to Felicity. With a graceful bow he said, "You must forgive Anthony's deplorable lack of manners. *I* am also Lady Meecham's nephew—Harold Eastcott—and I do not, I assure you, begrudge any expenditures she has made on your account."

Her colour heightened, Felicity replied, "And I . . . I am Miss Felicity Lyford." She paused, then forced herself to go on, "I . . . I don't quite know what to say to . . . to either of you."

"It don't signify," Eastcott assured her gracefully. "I can see that my cousin has put you out of countenance and I am determined to make amends. Won't you be seated, Miss Lyford?"

Gratefully, Felicity smiled and did as Lord Eastcott suggested. As she did so, Woodhall cleared his throat and said to his cousin, "You take Miss Lyford's presence with admirable composure, Harry."

Harry turned to look at Sir Anthony and raised an eyebrow. "Do I, cousin? Really, you are remarkably naive today. Or hadn't you considered the probable connection between our dear aunt's will and her sponsorship of an eligible young lady . . . as I feel sure Miss Lyford will prove to be."

It was evident from Sir Anthony's startled expression that he had not. It was also evident, had either gentleman bothered to look at her, that Felicity was more distressed than ever. So distressed was she that she did not see Woodhall frown warningly at his cousin.

"Of course, dear Tony. Discretion. Always discretion!" Eastcott said irrepressibly. "And I should never forgive myself if I were to put Miss Lyford out of countenance." He turned to her, then, and said, once more all gallantry, "You must allow me to call on you often, my dear. It is so refreshing, you know, to meet a young lady new to London. You are new to London, are you not, Miss Lyford?"

Bewildered, Felicity could only nod. She was saved, however, from having to reply, by a voice from the doorway. "By all means, visit the girl, Harry."

"Lady Meecham!"

"Aunt Cora!"

Lord Eastcott was the first to recover. He strode

forward and kissed her on the cheek as he said, "However do you contrive to look younger, each time I see you?"

"Tush, boy!" she retorted severely but with a pleased smile. "No Spanish coin, *if* you please!"

Lady Meecham paused. Neither Woodhall's affronted expression nor Eastcott's lazy amusement nor Felicity's heightened colour were lost on her. So they had gotten off to a stormy start, had they? Well, she knew how to keep a light hand on the reins! Amused, Lady Meecham said aloud, "Felicity, pray fetch my shawl. The new one. You needn't hurry."

"Yes, ma'am," Felicity murmured, grateful for any excuse to escape the room.

When she was gone, Sir Anthony turned to his aunt and said, in quizzing accents, "Shawls?"

She gave a bark of laughter. "Well it did remove Miss Lyford from the room." Lady Meecham then indicated a pair of chairs and added, "Sit down, both of you, for I mean to, and I can't abide looking up at people!"

With a crooked smile, Sir Anthony obeyed. As he did so, he studied his aunt for signs that Miss Lyford's visit was too tiring for her. Instead, he found to his surprise that she looked far better than he had seen her in some time. Lady Meecham wore a new dress of lavender and her grey hair, under a rather fetching cap, was curled to frame her face. Cora, aware of his scrutiny, said dryly, "Did you expect to find me all done up, nephew? I daresay I look more rested than you. What have you been doing?"

Woodhall shrugged. "This and that. Visiting friends and such. If I seem burnt to a socket, it is from boredom and not dissipation, I assure you!"

This last was spoken rather defensively, but Cora only nodded. "I believe you, boy. Except when you're in one of your black spells, you're positively *respectable!*"

"Unlike me?" Eastcott hazarded outrageously. At her look of disapproval he laughed and said coaxingly, "How can you have supposed, ma'am, that any nephew of yours could be content to run tame playing propriety?"

Lady Meecham gave a short laugh but said severely, "So far as I recall, I was never considered *ramshackle!*"

"But then you had the misfortune to be female and therefore always hemmed about by footmen and maids and such," Lord Eastcott pointed out. "Given *my* opportunities, you might well have outshone me!"

Sir Anthony did not appear amused by this exchange. Impatiently he interrupted them. "I wish you will tell us, Aunt Cora, about Miss Lyford. All I know is that Henkley said she was staying with you."

Lady Meecham thumped her cane against the floor in patent anger. "Man's an old maid! Very well. You wish to know about Miss Lyford? I'll tell you. She's the daughter of Geoffrey Lyford. Aye, you may stare! He left her practically penniless."

"But surely. . . ." Sir Anthony paused and began again. "Oughtn't she to be in mourning? Surely it has not been above two months since Lyford passed away."

"He forbade it!" Lady Meecham said triumphantly. "Said he didn't believe in such barbaric customs and that his children was to go about enjoying themselves."

Woodhall had himself in hand again and refused to

be baited. Quietly he said, "That doesn't explain why Miss Lyford is *here*, Aunt Cora."

Reminiscing, Cora explained, "Because her mother, Vera, was a dear sweet girl and I was very fond of her. Then she married Geoffrey Lyford and he wouldn't let me set foot in his house. Kept her squirrelled away, in fact, at Lyford Park so that I saw her not above twice in twenty years. But we wrote to each other and Vera told me about her children. I was to have brought Felicity out, but Vera died before the girl was of age and Geoffrey Lyford wouldn't let me near his daughter. From what I've been able to gather, which is precious little since she won't speak against her father, Felicity has had an unpleasant time of it. Lyford couldn't bear to be reminded of his dead wife, so he rarely spoke to the girl and made no provision for her needs. Expected her, however, to take charge of the household and make him comfortable. As I said, it can't have been pleasant for the child."

"Good God, no, ma'am!" Sir Anthony answered, appalled. "It's good of you to bring her out and dower her."

"Fiddlesticks!" Cora snorted. "I'm being selfish! Hasn't it ever occurred to you that I might be bored? Felicity brightens up the place and even Tifton is smiling these days!"

"And I thought——"

"I know what you thought!" Lady Meecham snapped. "Did you really believe I had entered my dotage? Or that she had an eye on my fortune? No such thing! I've had trouble enough getting her to accept all the little trifles I wish to bestow on her!"

"A most unusual girl!" Harry interjected lazily.

"Aye, quite out of the common way!" Cora retorted, rounding on him. "Or hadn't you noticed?"

He had. Lord Eastcott had found Miss Lyford sufficiently fresh from the country to pique his jaded interest. Had she been the typical provincial, he would not have been so intrigued, but Harry was quick to note that her eyes met his with an engaging frankness that argued against either insipid shyness or brazen forwardness. And, of course, there was her undeniable beauty. Yes, even without his aunt's interest in the girl, Lord Eastcott would have been pleased to meet her. All he said aloud, however, was, "And you no doubt have plans for her?"

Unaccountably, Lady Meecham's eyes dropped and she toyed with the head of her cane as she said airily, "Oh, I expect I'll have no trouble finding some young fellow to take her off my hands. Someone quiet and respectable, I think. Well off, but neither wealthy nor titled, for even with the portion I'll give her, there's no sense looking too high. None of *your* set, of course! Felicity is far too sensible to take up with useless fribbles."

"Disapprove of us, do you?" Sir Anthony asked cordially.

"Oh, I neither approve nor disapprove. It simply never occurred to me that either of you would be interested," she lied without hesitation.

Lord Harry could no longer contain his amusement and he laughed. "Doing it much too brown, my dear aunt! I've already told Tony my opinion . . . that you've imported the chit for *our* benefit, in hopes that one of *us* will toss her the handkerchief. She's not quite our style, of course," he added reflectively, "but I expect that's partly why you chose her." Eastcott paused and Lady Meecham favoured him with an evil stare that made him laugh. "Oh, don't worry, dear aunt! I've not the slightest objection to your scheme! I even rather admire it. I make no promises, mind you, but I've no objection to furthering my acquaintance with Miss Lyford." He paused again before he added, "I fancy she was not entirely indifferent to me."

"Coxcomb!" Cora snorted. She did not, however, look displeased.

In a carefully toneless voice, Sir Anthony asked, "And what is Miss Lyford's opinion of your delightful scheme, Aunt Cora? Or haven't you told her?"

Lady Meecham frowned at her nephew and snapped, "Felicity is a sensible girl and I don't expect she would turn down an offer as flattering as one from either of you."

It was evident that Sir Anthony wished to protest further but could not, for at that moment Felicity returned with the shawl. Rather shyly she took a seat at Lady Meecham's command and the discussion became general, with the three elder members exchanging the latest *on-dits*. Thus, for the first time, Felicity had the opportunity to study his lordship. Harry Eastcott was fair, unlike his cousin, with a rather stronger looking physique. His clothes, Felicity noted with wonder, seemed almost molded to his body and one could not imagine so much as a hair out of place. Lord Eastcott's shirtpoints were high, his neckcloth tied even more intricately than Sir Anthony's, and the few pins, fobs, and rings Eastcott wore were of the most elegant jewellers in town. Pleased by what she saw, Felicity found herself smiling more openly at his lordship, a circumstance not lost on Sir Anthony, who resolved to thrust a spoke into Aunt Cora's plans. For the moment, however, he contented himself with bearing Harry off with him a short time later.

Once her two nephews were gone, Lady Meecham demanded of Felicity, "Well? What did you think of 'em? And no roundaboutation, my girl! Pound dealings only."

"Very well, ma'am," Felicity answered, squaring her shoulders unconsciously. "To put the matter plainly, with no bark on it, I found Sir Anthony rude, arrogant, and insulting. If he were ever to smile I suppose one might call him handsome, but he did not for me. I found Lord Eastcott far more the gentleman. His manners and person were such as must please. Indeed, I find it difficult to credit my brother Richard's dislike of him."

"Found Anthony that bad, did you?" Lady Meecham asked thoughtfully.

Felicity hesitated, then her innate sense of justice made her smile and say, "I should have found him completely insupportable had he not been so rude out of concern for *you*, ma'am. He seems very fond of you."

With a touch of complaisance, Cora answered, "Both my nephews are very fond of me. As I am of them," she added sharply. "Never had children of my own, so I've had to enjoy other people's brats."

There seemed nothing to say to this and Felicity merely waited. It was a long wait, for Lady Meecham was lost in her own thoughts. Privately, she felt much encouraged. There was no denying that Felicity seemed taken with Harry, and he with her. As for Anthony, one might assume that his interest had, at the very least, been stirred. Now the question was how best to fan that interest? He was, of course, bound to keep meeting her. For one thing, Anthony had always run tame in Lady Meecham's home and was unlikely to stop merely because some chit of a girl was intruding. But that was the rub. Anthony might continue to feel Felicity was intruding. Ah, well, time enough to think about this later.

Felicity had no notion of the thoughts passing through Lady Meecham's head. It only seemed to her that her hostess was looking tired and she ventured to ask if Lady Meecham ought not to rest.

"Rest?" Cora snorted indignantly. "Do you think I'm in my dotage, child? We've invitations to write and send out! Nothing ambitious, you understand, merely cards, conversation, and food. And perhaps a small band should some of the young people wish to stand up to dance. It is of the first importance, my dear, that you be introduced to a few of the leaders of the ton. We'll be needing to procure vouchers for Almack's. To that end, I'll invite two of the Patronesses, who are my particular friends, and then it will be up to you to convince them you are worthy to be admitted to that place. *Not*, I fancy, that they would refuse anyone *I* have chosen to sponsor! So long as you don't do something foolish, such as waltzing before they have granted you permission, I anticipate no difficulty. The Lyfords, in spite of your father, are generally considered a most respectable family, and your mother was, after all, a Cavener."

Felicity listened quietly to these plans. It had taken her only a short time to realise that, even aside from her scheme for her nephews, Lady Meecham derived a good deal of pleasure from all the fuss that attended the launching of a young woman into society.

Nothing could be more delightful to her ladyship than all the shopping expeditions, conferences with hairdressers and modistes, and poring over lists of names of members of the ton and recollecting friendships. In her day, Lady Meecham had been a reigning belle and still felt most alive in the midst of a party. This realisation had gone a long way to reconciling Felicity to her equivocal position in Lady Meecham's household. For it was, in some ways, a difficult position. Felicity had no doubt that, were it general knowledge, Sir Anthony would not be the only one to condemn Felicity's situation. *That* reflection led to a feeling of mortification as Felicity wondered just what Lady Meecham had told her nephews. It had been galling to be sent out on a trumped-up excuse, but Felicity was obliged to admit that to have had to listen as Lady Meecham explained, in some fashion, her presence must have been even more painful.

Abruptly, Felicity realised that Lady Meecham was looking at her oddly. "I hope," Lady Meecham said severely, "that you are not subject to the megrims, my girl. *That* would be altogether unacceptable."

With a slight gurgle, Felicity laughed and assured her hostess, "I do not think, Lady Meecham, that I have ever been considered moody." Then, to distract her, added, "Shall I go and fetch the invitations? I should be happy to write them out for you."

Cora thumped her cane. "Trying to turn me up sweet, are you? Very well, I may as well get some work out of you. You'll find what you need in my writing desk; run along and fetch it."

IV

Rather to Felicity's surprise, Sir Anthony called again, two days later. Once more, Lady Meecham was out visiting friends. "You won't want to come with me," Cora had snorted. "Hetty's a dear soul, but older than I am and decidedly not young in her notions!"

So Felicity had acquiesced, aware that she ought, in any case, to devote the morning to writing a long letter to Richard. That project had been curtailed, however, when Felicity realised that she had very little to say to him. Even had she and Lady Meecham not, thus far, led such a quiet existence, Richard would disapprove of Felicity's devoting a letter to a description of frivolous pursuits. Sally might be interested in a discussion of the latest fashions, but Richard would not. Worldly nonsense, *he* would call it! Felicity sighed. She loved her brother dearly, but it could be such a trial dealing with someone who could not understand one's need for a little pleasure. In the end, Felicity had settled on a brief dutiful epistle and given it to Tifton to post. That left her at loose ends and she was in the drawing room when Sir Anthony was announced. Instinctively, Felicity smoothed her skirt as she waited for him to be shown up.

Sir Anthony paused at the doorway of the drawing room. "Good morning, Miss Lyford," he said politely. "Tifton informs me that my aunt has gone out?"

Felicity could not but feel a certain awkwardness in meeting Sir Anthony alone like this. She forced herself to smile, however, and say, "Why, yes, Lady Meecham went to visit a friend. Someone named Hetty, I believe. I'm afraid I can give you no notion of when she may return."

"Oh, well, it don't signify for actually I came to see you, Miss Lyford," was the astonishing reply.

Felicity stiffened. "Indeed, sir? Those words seem ominously familiar. Have you come to chafe at me again?"

Woodhall tilted back his head and laughed. "I beg pardon, Miss Lyford! I spoke without thinking!" he assured her genially. "So far from wishing to abuse you, I've come to take you for a drive. If you will come?" She hesitated and Sir Anthony went on coaxingly, "It's a lovely day outside, if a trifle cool, and I think you would enjoy the park. It will, in part, help me to atone for my rudeness the other day!"

There was, of course, but one answer one could give to that! "I shall be delighted," Felicity said, with a smile that matched his. "I must change, but you need not fear I shall keep your horses standing, for I can be ready in ten minutes."

If it was not ten minutes, it was certainly less than twenty before she stood in the entryway as Sir Anthony donned his riding coat with its sixteen capes. There were few men who could wear that particular garment of fashion without appearing rather ridiculous. Sir Anthony was one of them. Felicity herself wore a warm cloak and a fetching bonnet to protect her head. Sir Anthony, however, seemed scarcely to notice and Felicity found him once more aloof and unapproachable. Nevertheless, Felicity smiled at Sir Anthony in a determined fashion. The smile became more genuine when she saw his horses. They were matched chestnuts, but it was not this fact which drew her approval. Rather it was that they were, in her father's words, clearly a "bang-up set of cattle."

So impressed was Felicity that she halted in her tracks, causing Sir Anthony to say, with some asperity, "Well, Miss Lyford? Do you dislike my horses?"

She cast him a withering look. "I should be a flat if I did! You appear to be an excellent judge of horse-flesh, Sir Anthony. That is, if these chestnuts are your choice?"

Torn between exasperation and amusement, Woodhall retorted, "They are. And I am much obliged for your good opinion. I cannot tell you how it reassures me!"

In spite of herself, Felicity gave a gurgle of laughter. "It is too bad of me to speak with such condescension, isn't it?" she said. "And I ought to apologise. The thing is, you see, my father was very fond of horses and his stable was held to be exceptional."

As he handed Felicity into the curricle, Sir Anthony said quietly, "Yes, your father's horses were famous. I collect he taught you all about them?"

Woodhall was, by now, engaged in threading his way through the crowded street and therefore Felicity was not obliged to answer at once. When she did so, it was with a marked degree of reserve. "No, it was not my father who taught me about horses, Sir Anthony. It was our groom, Roberts. He also was the one who taught me how to ride and drive a carriage. Though I had little opportunity to handle the ribbons until after my mother died. Then, of necessity, I had a great deal."

Woodhall hesitated, then said, "I beg pardon if I have distressed you, Miss Lyford. My aunt has told me something of your circumstances and I collect you have not had an easy time of it."

Pity, however, was something Felicity was determined not to allow. "Your aunt has been all kindness to me, Sir Anthony, but I fear that an excess of kindness has made her exaggerate my . . . my difficulties."

This speech, spoken with such youthful pride, did not have quite the effect Felicity had intended. "*What?*" Sir Anthony demanded, in mock astonishment. "Do you mean to say that your life has been an endless round of parties? I have never been so deceived!"

Felicity laughed. "No, of course not! You are roasting me, sir. I only meant that the past is over and I do not choose to refine upon it. If I have had difficulties, so, too, have many other people. Mine have not been exceptional."

Privately, Woodhall disagreed but was too much the gentleman to press the point. He was, moreover, inclined to approve Miss Lyford's show of spirit. So it was that Sir Anthony gave Felicity one of his most engaging smiles as he said, softly, "Good girl!"

He was still smiling when they passed through the gates of the park. This, however, gave way to a *most* mischievous expression as Woodhall drew abreast of someone he knew. Aylesbury. "George! Hallo. May I present Miss Felicity Lyford? She's in London on a visit to my Aunt Cora. Miss Lyford, this is my friend George Aylesbury . . . an amiable if rather ramshackle fellow!"

Aylesbury cast his friend a withering look, then politely bowed to Felicity. "Your servant, ma'am."

Felicity murmured something unintelligible. Sir Anthony and Aylesbury exchanged a few words and then Woodhall set his curricle forward again. His next target proved to be a gentleman on horseback, who appeared as taken aback by Sir Anthony's unexpected civility as he was by the sight of Felicity. "Delighted, ma'am," he finally managed.

"How do you do?" Felicity responded, colouring faintly.

Suddenly, the full impact of what Woodhall had said penetrated the gentleman's consciousness and he asked, "Did you say Miss *Lyford?* Old Lyford's daughter?" Sir Anthony nodded and the gentleman said, "Well 'pon my soul! Heard Lyford was dead, but it must have been a mistake. What I mean is, stands to reason he can't be . . . Miss Lyford ain't in mourning!"

Felicity felt that nothing more was wanting to set the seal on her embarrassment. Quietly she said, "Geoffrey Lyford was my father and he is indeed dead. He did not believe in the custom of mourning and forbade us to follow it. You must know, sir, that whatever my own inclinations may have been, I felt myself bound to honour his wishes."

"Well done!" Woodhall whispered, so softly that Felicity could not be certain he had spoken. Then, rather haughtily, Sir Anthony said, "You must realise,

Cranslow, that it cannot be pleasant for Miss Lyford to answer these questions!"

"Quite so!" the poor fellow confirmed hastily. "Beg pardon, Miss Lyford! Tongue always running away with me. Tell you what. I could set it about, the story of why you're not in mourning, then you needn't have everyone quizzing you about it."

"What an excellent notion," Sir Anthony said amiably. "I wonder I didn't think of it!"

Cranslow puffed out his chest ever so slightly. "Glad to be of service. Don't fret now, Miss Lyford, I'll take care of the matter! I fancy anyone can tell you that Reginald Cranslow is a man to be depended upon. Well, best be on my way. Pleasure to have met you, Miss Lyford!"

They parted company and almost at once Sir Anthony heard the gurgle of laughter that had so delighted him earlier. With a cheerful grin, he looked down at Felicity. "Abominable child! What is there to amuse you about Cranslow? He is, I assure you, a *most* respectable man."

"I don't doubt it!" she retorted. Then, a puzzled frown replacing her smile, Felicity said, "You know, I have the oddest notion that you did not ask me to come out driving with you simply for the pleasure of my company." As Woodhall hesitated, a faintly sheepish expression on his face, Felicity rounded on him. "Now I have it! You are still angry with me for . . . for battening onto your aunt and you've decided to embarrass me at every possible turn!"

This was so far from Sir Anthony's intentions that he gave a shout of laughter, something his horses took exception to. When he had them back under control, Woodhall said, his voice quivering with amusement,

"Is that really what you think of me? You are wrong, you know! I brought you out driving to help you." At her sceptical expression, Sir Anthony assured Felicity, "It's true, Miss Lyford. As I understand the matter, my Aunt Cora invited you to stay with her for the Season. I presume the purpose of this visit is to help you find a husband? Well, I am only doing my best to help you by introducing you to as many eligible young men as possible!"

"I . . . I see," Felicity answered in a hollow voice.

She ought, she knew, to feel grateful. Certainly she should feel relieved that Sir Anthony appeared not to know of his aunt's scheme. But he did know, she recalled. Lord Eastcott had told him.

"Good!" Woodhall's brisk tone ruthlessly shattered her withdrawal. "Prepare yourself to be embarrassed once more, Miss Lyford . . . I see another friend of mine!"

In the next three-quarters of an hour, Felicity was introduced to no less than eight eligible young men of the ton. All were most complimentary and most grateful to Sir Anthony for the introduction. Such treatment could not but please, and soon Felicity had recovered her poise.

Most of these gentlemen were Sir Anthony's friends. As he was about to leave the park, however, he recalled his aunt's comments on the subject of "useless fribbles" and looked about him for a serious young man. Then his gaze alighted on Mr. Philip Crofton and he reined in, a devilish gleam in his eyes. "Hallo, Crofton, nice day!"

Crofton immediately recognised the driver of the curricle and he stiffened with evident distaste. The fact that Sir Anthony appeared to have a very attrac-

tive female beside him in no way mitigated Mr. Crofton's feelings. Nevertheless, he said politely, "Good
day, Sir Anthony."

Mischievously Woodhall said, "May I present Miss
Felicity Lyford to you, Crofton? She is, I assure you,
absolutely respectable in spite of her presence in my
curricle. She is staying with my Aunt Cora, who has
given me strict orders not to corrupt the girl!"

The effect of this speech was to render both Felicity and Mr. Crofton a deep crimson. Mr. Crofton
recovered first. Ignoring Woodhall, Philip said, "May
I welcome you to London, Miss Lyford? I collect you
have only recently come here?"

Felicity seethed with indignation at Sir Anthony's
outrageous behaviour. Determined to show him she
was not so easily put out of countenance, Felicity
turned coldly away from Woodhall and gave Crofton
her warmest smile. "How do you do, sir? And you're
quite right—I've been here no more than a month. Before that I was accustomed to live in the country and
I find London something of a shock."

"A pleasant one?" Woodhall asked goadingly.

"For the most part, why yes," Felicity answered
frankly. Then, succumbing to a mischievous impulse
of her own, she added, "Except that I find myself
quite eclipsed by the company I am keeping."

Sir Anthony ignored this sally, but Crofton replied
gallantly, "Impossible, Miss Lyford! I prophesize that
you will take the ton by storm this Season, and outshine us all!"

"Storm?" Sir Anthony said musingly. "I wonder
whether he has in mind the tornado or the hurricane?"

Felicity tried to control herself, but it was of no use
and the gurgle of laughter escaped her just as Mr.

Crofton was about to remonstrate with Sir Anthony. He stopped and, his countenance outraged, Mr. Crofton bowed coldly to the pair and walked away. Immediately, Sir Anthony headed his horses toward home. All contrition, Felicity said in a small voice, "That poor man!"

Woodhall spared a moment to look down at her quizzically. "Do you care?" He saw that she did and asked abruptly, "Did you like him, then?"

Felicity chose her words carefully. "Why, I found him neatly dressed, with the air of a courteous well-bred young man. And in spite of his evident dislike of you, Mr. Crofton was able to perceive my distress and try to ease it. There is, moreover, something about Mr. Crofton which reminds me of my eldest brother, Richard."

"I see. For my part, I find him a dead bore, don't you?"

The urge to goad Sir Anthony further was irresistible. Felicity looked down to hide her face and said innocently, "Why, how could I find Mr. Crofton a bore when he pays me such lovely compliments?"

Unaccountably, Sir Anthony found himself taking a very *long* route back to Lady Meecham's townhouse. His grip tight on the reins, he demanded, "Is that what you want, then, Miss Lyford? To be paid pretty compliments? Be assured there will be any number of men who will be happy to oblige you! I cannot, however, think it the best way to choose a husband."

"Oh, you may be sure, Sir Anthony, that when I marry, it will be to a man of *character*," she replied airily.

"Thank you!" Woodhall said grimly. "I know how I

may take that! My aunt has told me that you are too sensible a young woman to approve of such frivolous fellows as my friends and myself! I wonder you even consented to go out driving with me!"

There was a pause before Felicity answered, "But how could I refuse? I am quite certain it will add to my credit to be seen with you."

For a moment the matter hung in the balance, then a muscle in Sir Anthony's cheek quivered and he gave way to laughter. As did Felicity. Eventually, Sir Anthony said appreciatively, "Now I understand why you are not yet married, Miss Lyford. All of your suitors tried to strangle you and you took exception to their manners!"

Felicity laughed again and said, "How unhandsome of you, Sir Anthony! To take such advantage of a poor helpless young lady."

"I have never known any girl I would be less inclined to call helpless," Woodhall retorted instantly. "And that includes my Aunt Cora."

"Oh I don't know," Felicity said reflectively. "Lady Meecham has money and one ought not to discount the advantage that gives her."

"You, my abominable wretch, need no advantage!" he countered. Woodhall hesitated, then said, abruptly serious, "Actually I wish you *will* tell me why you haven't married. You must be close upon twenty, I should say. And even though you were kept on your father's estate, did you never meet any men?"

Felicity's hands gripped each other tightly inside her muff and it was with difficulty that she kept her voice steady. "Why, yes, several of my father's friends were looking about for wives. I could not feel, however, that I wished to be married to someone more than twice my age."

"Were there no *young* men?" Woodhall asked incredulously.

Her voice strained, Felicity answered, "A few. There were even, I suppose, one or two who would have taken me penniless. My father, however, refused all such offers and forbade them to see me again."

"Was he *mad?*" Sir Anthony asked. "I should have thought he would have been delighted to have you off his hands."

Felicity laughed grimly. "There *was* one man my father would have permitted me to marry. Lord Sterne. He held, you see, most of my father's gambling chits and my father was delighted when Lord Sterne expressed a desire for my hand. They both thought it a reasonable exchange . . . me in return for fifty thousand pounds of debt cancelled."

"Good God! *Sterne!*"

"Precisely. I should, I suppose, have been flattered that his lordship put such a high value on me, but I could not bring myself to accept. Have you ever met Sterne, Sir Anthony?" she ended naively.

His jaw set tight, Woodhall replied curtly, "I have. And he's no husband for a young girl."

"Well, I could not like him," Felicity said simply. Then, as her voice returned to normal, she added, "Fortunately, I am extremely strong-willed and even my father came to understand that nothing would prevail upon me to marry Lord Sterne. I believe it was four months until he spoke to me again," Felicity concluded meditatively.

With a good deal of constraint in his voice, Sir Anthony said, "And after your father died? Did none of your suitors return?"

Felicity looked straight ahead as she answered bluntly, "They were married or betrothed to someone else, by then. Even," she added with relish, "Lord Sterne."

"I'm sorry. Had you ... had you a *tendre* for anyone?" he probed.

Felicity shook her head. "No, my heart was untouched. I might have accepted Avenell, and I daresay we would have managed to rub along tolerably well together, but my heart was not touched." Woodhall did not reply and, after a few moments, Felicity rallied him, "What? Nothing to say, Sir Anthony? You are, no doubt, stunned to find yourself so deceived in me ... to find I am not the meek creature you thought me!"

"Baggage!" Sir Anthony retorted cheerfully, though his face was still set in a grim expression.

"Ah, I am wrong!" Felicity said with an air of reflection. "You feel I lack resolution. I should have bribed my maid to lend me her clothes, crept out of the house at midnight, and set off to make my fortune. Perhaps as a scullery maid? Or upon the stage? I did think of it, you know," she said wistfully, "but my dreary common sense kept intruding with all sorts of difficulties. So, in the end, I only stayed at home."

Felicity ended with a sigh which prompted Woodhall to say acidly, "I should hope so! Do give over such nonsense, Miss Lyford!"

"All right," she said agreeably.. Then, innocently, said, "Shall I ask you, instead, why *you* have never married?"

Sir Anthony pulled up his horses and, holding the reins tightly in one hand, he looked down at Felicity. "Miss Lyford," he said with feeling, "I am beginning to regret that I ever had the impertinence to ask you such a question!"

Felicity laughed. "How unfair of you, sir, to take away my excuse to be rude."

"Baggage!" he repeated. Then, as he urged his horses forward in a brisk trot, he added, "For once, Miss Lyford, I expect to enjoy a London Season. Until, that is, one of your suitors murders you, which, believe me, is inevitable!"

Felicity only laughed and told Sir Anthony to mind his cattle, a totally unnecessary reminder as he acidly informed her. All too soon, he set her down at Lady Meecham's door. "I shan't come up," he apologised, "as I've an appointment. Instead, I trust you to convey my compliments to my aunt!"

"I shall. And . . . and thank you, Sir Anthony. It was a most . . . a most agreeable drive," Felicity concluded, in her most grown-up voice.

Woodhall looked at her quizzically. "*Agreeable?* Come, come, Miss Lyford! Telling such whiskers! Interesting . . . unusual . . . exhilarating, these I might allow. But agreeable?"

Felicity's eyes twinkled delightfully as she laughed. Then, with a parting wave of her hand, she ran up the steps. Tifton was waiting for her and, as he took her hat, informed Felicity that Lady Meecham wished to see her in the drawing room.

Just as Lady Meecham subjected Felicity to a catechism of the morning's events, so, too, did Aylesbury tax his friend Sir Anthony sometime later that day. "You can't expect me not to want to know what it's all about!" Aylesbury informed his friend severely.

Woodhall laughed and tossed off the rest of his glass of wine. "Very well. Miss Lyford is my aunt's goddaughter and Lady Meecham is bringing her out this Season."

"That ain't all to it," George retorted. "Wouldn't have bothered yourself with her, if it was."

Sir Anthony frowned and shrugged. Impossible to divulge, even to so good a friend as Aylesbury, Miss Lyford's precise circumstances or Lady Meecham's scheme. "Let us say I was in a generous mood," Woodhall said finally.

Aylesbury knew Sir Anthony well enough to know that it was useless to ask any further questions. Instead, he observed casually, "Devilish attractive girl, Miss Lyford."

"Ummm," Woodhall agreed absently.

"Couldn't help thinking she was a bit more in your style than Miss Lucinda Carrington."

This brought Sir Anthony upright with a start. Favouring his friend with a determined stare, he said, "Let me make it quite clear, George, that there is no question of *that!* I was merely being agreeable to a guest of my aunt."

"Of course, dear boy," Aylesbury agreed blandly. "Of course. My lamentable tongue! Always running away with me, you know."

"I do know it," Sir Anthony said, rising.

"Hey! Where you going?" Aylesbury demanded. "Wasn't we to meet Ratherton here?"

"I've changed my mind," Woodhall answered. "I think I'll call on Miss Carrington instead."

"But what am I to tell Ratherton?" Aylesbury demanded, aggrieved.

"Anything you wish, dear boy, anything you wish," was the heartless reply.

V

When Sir Anthony arrived at the Carrington house-hold, he was greeted amiably by the butler. "Good to see you, sir. Miss Lucinda is in the Yellow Saloon. Shall I announce you?"

"Thank you, Kendal, but I'll announce myself."

This sort of breach of etiquette was, in Lady Carrington's eyes, forgiveable in very few persons. Sir Anthony and his cousin Lord Eastcott were among them. Indeed, considering that this was Lucinda's fifth Season and Lady Carrington still had hopes of bringing Sir Anthony to the point of declaring himself, she would have forgiven Woodhall much worse breaches of etiquette than that! Kendal was well aware of her ladyship's feelings in the matter, and therefore made no demure as Woodhall mounted the steps to the second floor.

As usual, Sir Anthony found Miss Carrington surrounded by half a dozen young men. At the sight of him, she smiled a welcome but did not let her gaze linger. She laughed, instead, at something someone beside her was saying and left Woodhall to make his way to a chair near her. One of the young men called to Sir Anthony, "Woodhall! Tell us your opinion of Miss C's portrait."

"Yes, Tony, pray do," drawled a familiar voice.

Lord Eastcott was sprawled negligently in a chair, apparently unconcerned that he had failed to obtain a place at the fair Lucinda's side. His eyes were twinkling at Sir Anthony, who turned to study the painting. After several minutes of absolute silence, Woodhall shrugged and said, "Oh, well, I cannot like it."

"Why not?" Lady Carrington asked, in her cool well-bred voice.

Sir Anthony looked at Lucinda, who was staring at him expectantly, and the thought came to him that she had never looked so lovely. From the top of her abundant blond curls to the tip of her dainty toes, Miss Lucinda's figure was perfection. It might have been expressly designed to show to advantage in the present fashion of sprig muslin dresses caught up below the bosom with ribbons. Her features, moreover, were delightful, with the blue eyes, pert little nose, and moist, rosebud mouth. With a hint of laughter, Sir Anthony answered, "Why, because it fails to capture all of Miss Carrington's beauty!"

With an engaging smile, Lucinda retorted, "And *I* think you are roasting me, sir! It is generally held to be an excellent likeness."

He pretended to study again the newly-hung painting. Finally he said, with a sigh, "The difficulty is, you see, that I have such a fondness for the original."

She laughed, but shook her head at him. "How can I believe you, Sir Anthony, when I have it on the best authority that just this very morning you were out driving with another young lady?"

Sir Anthony frowned. "Why, so I was. My aunt's goddaughter. Are you jealous?"

Whatever her feelings, Lucinda Carrington was too clever to answer such a question. Lord Eastcott chose that moment to say, maliciously, "She is quite young, and quite attractive, Miss C."

"Is she?" someone else asked.

This time Sir Anthony shrugged. "Oh, without a doubt."

"Perhaps I ought to make her acquaintance," Lucinda said provocatively, "if you find her so attractive."

"By all means," Woodhall replied coolly. "I feel it my responsibility to warn you, however, that what Miss Lyford lacks in years she makes up for in devastating frankness!"

"Sounds almost as if you dislike the girl," someone said with a laugh.

"Perhaps it is rather Miss Lyford who dislikes, or at any rate disapproves of, Sir Anthony," Eastcott offered softly.

"Does she really?" The speaker was awed. "Is she queer in the attic? Someone said she was Geoffrey Lyford's daughter, so why——"

Sir Anthony cut him short ruthlessly. "*That* is precisely why Miss Lyford disapproves of me, I fancy. Under the circumstances, one can see that she might feel wary of anyone she thinks might be of her father's sort. And no, Bardolf, so far as I know, she is not queer in the attic. Quite the contrary. I found her to possess an excess of common sense!"

Lucinda, who disliked having the company's attention so thoroughly turned away from herself, now said, almost purring, "*I* should never disapprove of you, Sir Anthony!"

"What? Never?" he asked, with some amusement.

Demurely she lowered her lashes and smiled. Woodhall eyed her speculatively and then said, "I wonder if I should consider that a challenge, Miss Carrington?" Her eyes immediately flew to his face in alarm and he laughed. "Calm yourself, my dear. I was only roasting you."

Lady Carrington, seated on the far side of the room with her needlework, judged it time to intervene. With apparent severity she said, "I do not find such jests amusing, Sir Anthony."

Woodhall, though not deceived, found that he was growing restless, so he seized the opportunity to say, "Indeed? How unfortunate! You will no doubt be pleased, then, to learn I am leaving."

"But you've just now come!" Lucinda protested angrily. "You can't want to leave yet!"

Even Lady Carrington showed a trace of alarm, but Sir Anthony was adamant. "I must go. Though how you could imagine I *wish* to is beyond me!"

Lucinda smiled but said coolly, "Very well, go! We shall manage quite well without you."

As he rose to his feet, Sir Anthony answered obscurely, "I don't doubt it." Then, smoothly, "Good day, Lady Carrington. Gentlemen."

Downstairs, Sir Anthony found that his cousin Eastcott intended to join him. "Walk with me as far as White's," Harry said coaxingly.

"What makes you think I'm going there?" Woodhall countered.

"I don't. But I am, and I wish to speak with you," Eastcott answered cheerfully.

Sir Anthony laughed. "Very well, but only as far as White's!"

He then waited patiently for Harry to broach what was on his mind. Eastcott, however, was in no hurry. After several minutes, he did say, "That was not very adroit of you, Tony, back there. If you're not careful, you may lose the fair Lucinda."

Sir Anthony shrugged impatiently. "Oh, I think not. Miss Carrington is a sensible young woman and should I choose to toss her the handkerchief, I cannot think she would refuse. Nevertheless, you are right and I was maladroit. You may be sure that next time I shall exercise more care."

"Such arrogance!" Eastcott murmured. He seemed thoughtful, however, and after several more minutes he said, "You seem a bit out of curl, Tony. And reflection leads me to ask if your mood has anything to do with our aunt's guest?" Aware that his cousin had no intention of answering, Eastcott went on, "I wish you will tell me why you did take Miss Lyford about. Surely not to fix your interest with her? Particularly as I understand you made it a point to introduce her to every eligible gentleman you saw."

Sir Anthony smiled grimly. "How perceptive of you, Harry. No, I was merely trying to do the child a good turn, *not* fix my interest with her, as you so crudely put it. Tell me, Harry, doesn't it offend your pride to have Aunt Cora dangle the chit before our noses like this?"

Eastcott shook his head and sighed. "Now that, Tony, is the difference between us. *I* am a practical man and have discarded the luxury of pride."

With a frown, Woodhall abruptly said, "I thought you to have decided on Miss Carrington."

Lord Eastcott flicked an imaginary piece of lint from his sleeve as he said off-handedly, "Alas, Miss Carrington is quite lovely, but she begins to grow so predictable. It appears, moreover, that in spite of Aunt Cora's will—and why not—Lucinda is still inclined to favour you over the rest of us poor mortals. I should dislike to arrive, someday, with my poor tribute of flowers, a fan, or whatever, only to be informed she is betrothed to you."

A trifle grimly, Sir Anthony said, "I anticipate Miss Lyford will have at least as many suitors as Lucinda."

"But you will not be among them?"

"No, I will not be among them," Woodhall concurred.

Eastcott nodded, apparently satisfied. "Tell me, Tony. Did Miss Lyford appear to favour any of the gentlemen you introduced her to this morning?"

Woodhall took malicious pleasure in his reply. "Why, yes, she did seem to like Crofton."

"*Crofton?*" Lord Eastcott said in strong accents of loathing. "Philip Crofton? That . . . that *puritan?*"

"He paid her some very pretty compliments," Woodhall added with an air of innocence.

Lord Eastcott halted in his tracks. "Now that, Tony, is coming it too strong. Pretty compliments, indeed! You are roasting me and I refuse to regard anything you say."

Sir Anthony shrugged. "As you will, but do come along. You are making a spectacle of us!"

Harry realised the justice of this admonition and began walking in the direction of White's again. After a few moments' reflection, he said, "Crofton, eh? Well, I shan't regard it. Pretty fellows we should be if we can't outshine that lack-'o-joy!"

"I don't mean to try," Sir Anthony retorted curtly. "But if you choose to do so, I wish you luck."

Witheringly, Eastcott responded, "No you don't, Tony. You wish Miss Lyford will give me a terrible setdown, don't you? Shall we make a small wager on the matter?"

Haughtily, Sir Anthony replied, "I never wager on a young lady's inclinations!"

Not in the least offended or abashed, Harry laughed and said, "Wise fellow!"

In spite of himself, Sir Anthony grinned. He was relieved to see, however, that they had reached Eastcott's destination. "Join me?" Harry offered affably.

Woodhall shook his head. "No, I've business to attend to at home. Perhaps another time."

"I doubt it," Harry retorted with a lazy grin. "I won't, however, try to keep you. Good day, cousin."

"Good day, Harry!"

A short time later Sir Anthony strode down the hallway of his house toward the library feeling that nothing more could possibly go wrong. His hat, gloves, and coat had literally been thrown at poor Parr, his butler. And yet, Sir Anthony would have been hard-pressed to explain just what had put him in such a foul mood, he only knew he felt thoroughly out of sorts. Nevertheless, Woodhall was not a man to shirk his responsibilities and he would begin with the day's mail. As always, it had been placed on a silver salver on the desk in Sir Anthony's library. This was, most clearly, a man's room. Dark panelling, solid uncompromising pieces of furniture, burgundy carpet and hangings, as well as the rows upon rows of books had certainly led Lady Woodhall, Sir Anthony's mother, to avoid it. It was also Sir Anthony's favourite room in the house.

Now, seating himself at his desk, Sir Anthony began to sort through the mail. There were, of course, the usual invitations. London was yet relatively deserted by the ton, but those hostesses still present must consider Sir Anthony Woodhall a desirable guest. Either one had daughters to bring to his attention or one found him delightful to flirt with oneself, for there were few women in London impervious to Sir Anthony's charm. When he chose to exert it. It was, perhaps, this propensity to flirt, coupled with a superb discretion, that had led to Woodhall's mistaken reputation as a rake. It was generally agreed that a man who flirted so outrageously and who had so many blatant invitations cast up at him, could not possibly be celibate. Nor was he. But Sir Anthony had conducted his affairs with such exquisite discretion that not the most persistently inquisitive persons had been able to discover *where* he had bestowed his favours. Thus the members of the ton had been forced to fall back on gossip and speculation, and the number of his conquests was vastly overestimated.

Of these invitations, the one that drew Sir Anthony's attention first was Lady Meecham's. He immediately understood its significance. So Aunt Cora was about to introduce Miss Lyford to Society. Good. Provided the girl remembered to keep a rein on her tongue, this informal party ought to do the trick nicely. It was just the sort of evening that Sir Anthony was inclined to consider a dead bore, but he had resigned himself to attending with surprising ease when he discovered a letter among the other invitations. It was from his bailiff at Woodhall Manor. A quick perusal of the missive served to inform Sir Anthony that he would have to go there, himself, to settle the matter. Rather annoyed, he tried to decide just how long he would have to be gone. Long enough to miss Aunt Cora's party, he realised with regret. Nor could the matter be postponed until after Lady Meecham's party. Finally, Woodhall shrugged. His presence, after all, was not essential to her ladyship. Later in the Season, no doubt, someone would need to keep an eye upon Miss Lyford's suitors to see if there were any she need be warned about. But so early in the year it could not be expected that she would attract a great deal of attention, in spite of his and his aunt's best efforts. As for Aunt Cora, Tifton knew precisely how to order the household for a party in order to take most of the responsibilities away from Lady Meecham's shoulders. There were, moreover, one or two of her *cicisbei* who were certain to lend their masculine support on the evening in question.

It was, therefore, with a relatively clear conscience that Sir Anthony sat down to write a note to his aunt explaining his expected absence at her party. This was followed by a rather more flowery epistle to Miss Lucinda Carrington which extended his apologies, *in advance*, for neglecting her. With some amusement, Sir Anthony sealed the latter note. He had no doubt that Lucinda and her mother would misinterpret it and assume that he had been genuinely piqued, earlier, and had chosen this method of repaying them. Indeed, he had no doubt that he would return to London to find Miss Carrington and her mother all graciousness toward him. Sir Anthony frowned. Eastcott had said that Lucinda was becoming predictable.

To his annoyance, Sir Anthony realized it was true. This thought was followed by the question of whether that was good or bad. Surely it would be desireable to have a wife one understood? Why should any man *wish* to spend his life wondering what the woman he lived with would say or do next? Of all people, he ought to know the drawbacks of that! Unhappily for his peace of mind, however, Sir Anthony also found himself wondering if boredom might not be at least as unenviable a state. Unable to resolve the question, Sir Anthony, in the end, chose to evade it. A footman was summoned to carry the letters to his aunt and to Miss Carrington and Sir Anthony repaired upstairs to inform his valet that they would leave in the morning for Woodhall Manor.

VI

As Sir Anthony had predicted, Tifton knew how to arrange matters to a nicety. It was he who ordered the flowers and wine and saw to it that the rooms were set in order. He knew precisely how many tables ought to be set out and whether one ought to serve a punch, nor was the task of hiring extra link-boys beyond his power. The morning of the party he spent supervising the polishing of Lady Meecham's silver, the setting out of the best crystal, and the activities of the kitchen, for Tifton would leave nothing to chance. Upstairs, Felicity was engaged in reassuring Lady Meecham that all was well in hand and that she need fear no mishap for, although Cora was generally a most self-assured woman, she had the unfortunate tendency to become overset whenever she gave a party. And, as she grew nervous, so too did Lady Meecham become short-tempered. "Anthony knows how I feel!" she told Felicity with an air of injury. "I am sure he could have been present had he only made the attempt! As for Harold, he has the audacity to coolly inform me he may arrive late."

Felicity tried to answer soothingly. "Well, but General Sutcliffe has promised to come early, and Roxbury, too."

Cora sniffed. "That is *not* the same as having one's nephews!"

Felicity laughed and retorted, "Very true! Were it merely Sir Anthony and Lord Eastcott at your side, no one would be able to say how indecent it was that you should have so many admirers dangling after you, at your age."

"*Faradiddles!*" Cora answered sharply. It was plain, however, that the notion had taken and would go far to reconcile Lady Meecham to the situation. Complacently, she smiled at her image in the mirror, then turned to Felicity and said querulously, "I wish you will go see to Tifton. He cannot be trusted to manage the simplest of affairs!"

"Certainly, ma'am," Felicity said, immediately rising. "I'll check on him at once."

It was, Felicity knew, the most outrageous slander, for she was well aware how busy Tifton had been the past few days, and how efficient. Her own nerves, however, were rapidly fraying and she had been grateful for the opportunity to escape listening to Lady Meecham's fears. Once downstairs, Felicity contented herself with asking Tifton if there were anything she could do to help. Turning a fatherly smile on her, Tifton said, "Worriting, is she? No need for it, miss. Everything will be in order. As for helping, bless you, but there's nought but a bit more to be done and you may as well rest yourself for tonight."

Correctly interpreting this to mean that Tifton would be personally affronted if she persisted, Felicity hastily withdrew abovestairs to her own room. She felt no need of rest and would have preferred to take a brisk walk, but Lady Meecham would have viewed such an exercise as an act of desertion. Felicity contented herself instead with mending the hem of one of her dresses. Ordinarily this would have been attended to by one of Lady Meecham's servants. But when her abigail protested, Felicity said, "Oh, Annie, pray don't stop me! It is not as though I have not done this sort of thing often enough, at home."

Crossing her arms, the older woman smiled sourly. "That's as may be, Miss Felicity, but there you had to. And unfair I always called it, when you wouldn't have needed to if your father hadn't been such a wild one!"

"Annie!" Felicity's tone was ominous.

But Annie would not retreat. "Begging your pardon, Miss Felicity, but it's true and well you know it! And I'll say so even if he is dead. Pleased I was, when her ladyship came and brought you back to London and dressed you as you ought to be dressed. Aye, and promised to bring you out as if you was her own kin. Which is why I don't like to see you doing such mending as you don't need to anymore."

"Yes, but I shall go mad, Annie, if I don't do something of the sort! Her ladyship is worrying herself so, over this party, that I daren't stir out of my room for fear of having to listen to her, and I'm too excited to rest!"

At this short speech, Annie's face softened and she said, "Aye, nervous, too, I'll be bound. Your first real party, for I don't count the times your father's friends visited Lyford Park."

Their eyes met in perfect understanding. Annie had been with the Lyfords for many years, for she had been hired to wait on Felicity's mother shortly after

the birth of her first child. So when Vera Lyford had
died, it had seemed natural for Felicity to turn to An-
nie for comfort and counsel. There was very little that
Annie Wallis did not know about her young mistress
or the circumstances that had brought Felicity to
London. She could not altogether approve of Lady
Meecham's scheme, though she was forced to admit
Felicity had had little enough choice in the matter.
Master Richard was a most . . . most estimable man,
but it would simply not do for Miss Felicity to make
her home with him. But it was, and had always been,
Annie's dream to see Miss Felicity fall in love with
some young man, *any* young man, who would marry
her and take care of her.

Felicity, watching the expressions flitting across her
abigail's face, had a tolerable notion of what Annie
was thinking. She laughed a little as she said, "Annie
Wallis! How dare you doubt that I shall be a success?
Why, already Mr. Philip Crofton has predicted I shall
take the ton by storm!"

"That's as may be." Annie concealed her pride behind an air of aloofness. "But it cannot be denied you
haven't a fortune to match your looks. Oh, I've no
doubt you'll have as many beaux as you want dangling after you, paying you compliments, but how
many will come up to scratch is another question."

Setting aside her sewing, Felicity said seriously, "I
know it, Annie. But *someone* must, for I find I cannot
bear the notion of living with Richard and Sally and
dwindling into an old maid, looking after the six or
ten children they will no doubt have."

"You were ready enough to become a governess
and look after someone else's children," Annie pointed
out.

Felicity laughed. "And you know you told me I should hate it! But don't you see? The two cases are quite different, though I own I should not be *happy* to seek a post as governess. But at least I should feel less dependent than if I were living with Richard, for I should be paid a wage, however paltry, and know I was earning my keep. What's more, my employers would see me that way and not as an impoverished relation who must be looked after."

"Well, tonight will tell us what we may hope for," Annie said philosophically. "I've no doubt her ladyship will fill her saloons and *you'll* be dressed as I would like you to be. Ten to one, no gentleman will be able to take his eyes off of you! Thank the lord her ladyship has an eye for fashion."

Later, left alone with her thoughts, Felicity recalled her trip to Giselle, the dressmaker. Lady Meecham had persuaded Felicity to choose a gown of silver and blue. The modiste had been enthusiastic in her agreement. It would be unexceptionable for a girl in her first Season and yet would set mademoiselle apart as someone to be noticed. She should, indeed she *must*, have the dress, and Giselle would pledge to have everything, but everything, ready in two days. Trust Giselle! She had just the slippers to wear with it, if mademoiselle would condescend to try them? She would, and the dress was purchased. Mademoiselle would be *ravissante!*

Such daydreams helped to pass the time. And, that evening, as she looked in the mirror, Felicity could not but be pleased with Giselle's handiwork. With her hair curled and dressed by Lady Meecham's own hairdresser (a great sacrifice), a circle of pearls about her neck, and wearing the dress, slippers, and

matching gauze shawl about her shoulders, Felicity
knew herself to look enchanting. "Though it is not,"
she told Annie with a twinkle in her eyes, "becoming
of me to say so."

Annie merely smiled sourly and adjured her young
charge to take herself off to Lady Meecham. Only
when Felicity was gone did she allow herself to sit
down and cry, quite overcome at the sight of her
young mistress looking, as she felt, quite like a fairy
princess!

Lady Meecham was, herself, formidably dressed in
purple satin with a turban on her head. It was the
first time Felicity had seen her ladyship wear a turban and she was not entirely able to suppress her astonishment. Fortunately Lady Meecham chose to be
amused. "Lord, girl, I know it's a sight! But im-
pressive, ain't it?" Felicity had to agree with that and
Lady Meecham added, "Well, I want to impress 'em,
tonight. I want 'em to be afraid to offend me. When
waging a battle, my dear, never neglect the heavy ar-
tillery! Now, let's go find Sutcliffe and Roxbury. Much
too old for you, but we'll see what they think."

Roxbury and Sutcliffe, waiting downstairs, were
suitably overwhelmed. The general bowed and said,
"Beautiful, ma'am! And how one is to choose between
the pair of you is beyond me."

He, himself, was splendid in court dress, as was
Roxbury, and it was rather playfully that Cora
reproved him. "Fie, Charles! I wish to know what you
think of Felicity."

Both Roxbury and Sutcliffe appeared to study the
matter. They were sensible men, inclined to seek the
company of women their own age, feeling that it
could only be absurd in them to pursue girls just out.

Particularly as they were of an age to appreciate good conversation more than a trim figure. Roxbury nevertheless gave it as his opinion, "Won't be surprised if you have her off your hands even before the Season begins, m'lady."

General Sutcliffe was more reserved. "She does you credit, my dear. Credit indeed!"

Neither lady could fail to feel flattered, and both felt the evening to have had a most auspicious beginning. Now that the moment had come to greet the first guests, Lady Meecham's fears were gone, replaced by her famous poise and clever tongue. She was the perfect hostess, condescending to honour those persons fortunate enough to be guests in her house.

And, indeed, Lady Meecham was considered a superb hostess. It was soon clear that all of the invitations sent out had been accepted. The guests, numbering not above fifty, were predominantly older, of course, and invited because they could help Felicity if they chose to do so. Lady Jersey and Princess Esterhazy might produce vouchers for the assemblies at Almack's. And Serena Marshall might offer to chaperone Felicity to those affairs too strenuous for Lady Meecham's health. The young men present were to serve either as foils to Sir Anthony and Lord Eastcott or as possible suitors, should her two scapegrace nephews fail to offer for Miss Lyford. Though how either boy could resist the girl, if they were to see her in such looks as she enjoyed tonight, was beyond Cora.

Actually, Lady Meecham owed more than she knew to Sir Anthony for the success of her party among the younger set. A typical reaction to the re-

ceipt of her invitation had been astonishment and an
instant inclination to avoid what must certainly be an
insipid evening. That, however, was before Miss Lyford's description had begun to spread about, and the
interesting information that Sir Anthony Woodhall
had been seen driving her about the park in his curricle. *Then,* their curiosity piqued, the gentlemen had
been inclined to consider themselves fortunate to
have the opportunity to steal a march on the rest of
the male members of the ton in pursuit of a new
Beauty. Nor, upon seeing Miss Lyford, were they disappointed. Her eyes sparkled with the excitement of
her first party and her colour was nicely heightened.
Lord Eastcott was not the only one to note that she
met ones eyes frankly. A diamond of the first water,
was the general consensus.

Lady Meecham noted with approval that Felicity
met the compliments she received becomingly. Some
girls, so inexperienced, would either have become
bold in an attempt to appear sophisticated or lapsed
into a tongue-tied silence. Felicity did neither, and if
she was in a fair way to having her head turned by
all this flattery, no one could have guessed it.

Lady Jersey and Princess Esterhazy arrived together and it was obvious to Cora that they had been
consulting on the question of Miss Felicity Lyford.
With a sinking sensation, Lady Meecham realised
that they had reached the point where, if one chose
to approve Felicity, the other was prepared to take
her in dislike. Nevertheless, Lady Meecham allowed
none of her dismay to show in her face. She continued to play the *grande dame* as she said, "Sally!
Princess! How delightful to see you. May I make my
protégée known to you? Lady Jersey, Princess Ester-

hazy, my goddaughter, Miss Felicity Lyford. Felicity, make your curtsey to the ladies."

As Felicity did so, the two Patronesses of Almack's surveyed her sharply. With a slight edge to her voice, Lady Jersey said, "Well, Miss Lyford. I suppose you have come to London to outshine us all?"

Feeling rather awed by this dashing lady, Felicity was betrayed into exclaiming, "I don't think it would be possible!"

Sally Jersey gave a sharp laugh, not altogether displeased by the implied compliment to herself. Even Princess Esterhazy permitted herself a slight smile. At least the girl was modest. Then, a trifle sternly, she demanded, "Why are you not in mourning, Miss Lyford? I collect you *are* Geoffrey Lyford's daughter?"

Although heartily sick of the question, Felicity had by now perfected her answer. Staring fixedly at the floor, she said, "It was my father's wish, ma'am, and after his death I could not bring myself to disobey it."

Both ladies raised their eyebrows but could find no fault with this reply. It was, after all, just the sort of thing Lyford would ask of his children! With unspoken mutual consent, both ladies inclined their heads, graciously, and swept away into the cardrooms. Cora gripped the bannister tightly and let out a deep breath. In a barely audible voice she said, "Well, child, you may yet see the inside of Almack's!"

Serena Marshall, who arrived a short time later, was also pleased. She pronounced herself charmed by Miss Lyford's sweet manners and pledged herself to chaperone Felicity to as many such affairs as she wished. Her own daughter was of much the same age and they would no doubt get on famously. Such a pity it was that Druscilla was pledged elsewhere, that evening.

Never mind that it was highly unlikely that Serena Marshall would have been so obliging had her daughter, Druscilla, not been firmly betrothed to a most eligible young man. It was still a gesture that would be of great benefit to Felicity, for Serena Marshall had the happy knack of being well liked by everyone. Even the stiffest of matrons would be unlikely to cast a cold shoulder on Felicity if she were introduced under Serena Marshall's auspices. Lady Meecham's triumph was complete.

It was perhaps this degree of success that allowed her to greet Lord Eastcott kindly even though his arrival was far later than she would have liked. Nor could Cora be pleased that he had brought Lucinda Carrington with him. Nevertheless, she managed a smile and a light reply to his apology. Then she addressed herself to Lady Carrington, who stood in front of her daughter Lucinda. "Alvinia! How delightful! And your daughter. She grows more lovely *each year.*"

Lady Carrington smiled thinly. "Such a relief, Cora, to know one need not worry about her. I mean, one could scarcely mistake *Lucinda* for a provincial who is not yet up to snuff."

Thus the battle lines were drawn and Lucinda stepped into the fray. She ignored Lady Meecham, who was bristling, and spoke to Felicity. "You must be Miss Lyford. Tony and Harry have solicited my kindness on your behalf. Having seen you, I do hope we shall be friends, Felicity."

"Of course, Lucinda," Felicity replied with a sweetness that deceived no one.

For a moment, the two young ladies stared at each other in open appraisal. Neither was pleased with what she saw. One was fair, one was dark. If Miss Carrington had the advantage in height, Miss Lyford must have been held to have the finer features. Felicity wore blue and silver, Lucinda foaming green. Lucinda was the more sophisticated, but Felicity held the lure of naiveté.

Lucinda broke the silence first. "You mustn't blame Sir Anthony or Lord Eastcott for mentioning you to me. We are so close, you see, that it is only natural that we share our concerns."

At this imprudent speech, Lady Carrington would have checked her daughter had she not seen that Lord Eastcott was far more amused than otherwise. Lady Meecham merely waited to see what Felicity would reply. With apparent surprise, Felicity answered, "Are you of an age with those gentlemen, then? I should have said you looked no more than five and twenty!"

Lord Eastcott gave a short bark of laughter as Lucinda snapped, "I'm twenty-three!" Then, hastily recollecting herself, she said, with a short laugh, "Sir Anthony did tell me about your devastating frankness, Miss Lyford. Perhaps I should warn you, since you have obviously been pitchforked into the ton with no notion how to go on, that gentlemen generally do not like such boldness in a woman."

"Oh, do you find they prefer to be toad-eaten?" Felicity asked softly.

Once more Lord Eastcott laughed as Lucinda struggled with her temper. "Certainly not! I merely meant that a certain civility is expected of a lady. I realize that living so isolated as you have, you must have had no chance to learn such things, Miss Lyford, and I warn you for your own good. Sir Anthony found you most impertinent!"

"Did he?" Felicity asked, a martial light appearing in her eyes. "Perhaps I found *him* impertinent."

Lady Carrington permitted herself a superior smile. "I think you will find, Miss Lyford, that the rest of society scarcely agrees with you. Sir Anthony said you had an excess of common sense and I understand that one of the nicknames that has already attached itself to you is Miss Practicality! I even understand there to be a rumour that Sir Anthony has left town expressly to avoid this party."

Tartly, Cora intervened, "Well, that's better than Ice Maiden! As for rumours, the one *I* heard was that his absence had more to do with Miss Carrington than with Felicity!"

The two elder ladies glared at one another as the two younger ones exchanged excessively sweet smiles. This prompted Lord Eastcott to bow and say, "I shall be a peacemaker and bear Miss Carrington off to find a glass of champagne!"

With an air of triumph, Lucinda seized the opportunity to escape, nor did Lady Carrington attempt to stop her. Not in the least pleased, Lady Meecham said acidly, "Really, Alvinia! I wonder you allow that girl to expose herself in front of Eastcott like that."

"And I wonder at you, Cora!" Lady Carrington retorted. "One cannot, after all, take these provincials and expect to turn them into perfect young ladies in a month or two!"

"How fortunate, then, that I've had no need to alter Felicity one whit," Lady Meecham said sweetly. "Nor have I any fear that *she* will end upon the shelf. Really, Alvinia, I cannot think what you are about, waiting so long to find a husband for Lucinda. One might almost think she had a squint!"

Lady Carrington turned a shade of purple that did not at all go well with the dark blue of her dress and felt herself on the point of apoplexy. There was nothing to do, however, except draw herself rigidly erect, bow majestically to Cora Meecham, and coldly continue up the steps to the drawing rooms. Felicity was barely able to repress a gurgle of laughter, a gurgle that fortunately passed unnoticed. Lady Meecham nevertheless eyed Felicity sharply and abruptly said, "Well, go on and enjoy yourself, child. I don't expect I'll need you any longer. There's no one left to arrive that signifies. Needn't warn you to guard your tongue, do I? And don't let that . . . that hussy provoke you!"

Demurely Felicity said, "Yes, ma'am."

Lady Meecham sighed. "Well, go on with you! You've got to begin somewhere."

Five rooms were devoted to Lady Meecham's party: two given over to cards, two given over to conversation, and one to food. Lady Meecham had decided against the musicians. By the time Felicity had been released from Lady Meecham's side, most of the elder guests had retired to the cardrooms leaving the younger set to chat among themselves as they wished. Lucinda, of course, was surrounded by young men, several of whom immediately detached themselves from her court and joined Felicity. "Fetch you an ice, Miss Lyford?" one gentleman offered.

"Or a glass of champagne," another said, with a disdainful look at the first fellow.

Felicity laughed and said recklessly, "Oh by all means let it be champagne!"

The glass was quickly fetched and Felicity took a sip. It was her first taste of champagne for Geoffrey Lyford, though careless in other ways, had declared that he refused to waste the stuff on a mere schoolroom chit who couldn't possibly appreciate it. A judgement Felicity now found herself forced to admit had been justified. Impossible, however, to allow these admiring young men to see that she disliked it, so Felicity smiled and took another sip.

Lord Eastcott, who stood nearby, had observed everything and he had a tolerably good idea of what Felicity was thinking. It amused him and, with an ease born of long practice, he joined the group and even contrived to place himself at Felicity's side. "Well, Miss Lyford, are you enjoying London?" he asked with a smile. "You are kept amused?"

Felicity looked at Lord Eastcott with rather mixed emotions. She had not seen him since the morning he had called upon Lady Meecham, and his absence had piqued her. As had the fact that he had arrived with Miss Carrington this evening. She felt Eastcott was laughing at her, yet there was a look of admiration in his eyes that could not fail to please her. With what she hoped was an off-handed air, Felicity finally said, "Overwhelmed more than amused, I should say, Lord Eastcott."

"Then, undoubtedly, you have had the wrong person showing you London!" Lord Eastcott laughed. "Let me take you about and I promise you you will come away feeling at ease and even entertained."

The other young gentlemen present were not amused. It could not be helped that Lord Eastcott held the advantage of being Lady Meecham's nephew, but need he use it so outrageously? A little taken aback by Eastcott's eagerness, Felicity only laughed and said, "Perhaps."

At this point, to everyone's surprise, Lady Jersey bore down on the group and placed a hand on Lord Eastcott's arm. "Harry!" she said reprovingly, "What are you doing? Trying to ruin Miss Lyford's reputation? You must know, Miss Lyford, that Harry is accounted a most dangerous rake! Come, instead, and amuse *me* Harry, with the latest *on-dits.*"

Lord Eastcott went with good grace. As soon as they were out of earshot of the group around Felicity, he demanded, "Now why, I wonder, did you do that, Sally?"

She laughed, "Charity, pure charity! How came Cora to be such a nodcock as to encourage *you* to dangle after the chit?"

Eastcott flicked a speck from his immaculate sleeve as he said carelessly, "Perhaps she would like to see me creditably settled."

"You?" Lady Jersey said with frank astonishment. "She must have windmills in her head!"

"Do you find the notion so odd?" Eastcott asked, a bitter note to his voice.

Lady Jersey eyed him speculatively. "Since you ask, yes . . . most odd. I also, however, have heard a certain rumour concerning Cora Meecham's will. I can only say that if she thinks marriage will be the making of you, she is more optimistic than I."

"Why, Sally, I thought you liked me!" he protested.

She laughed and tapped him with her fan. "And so I do, Harry. I find you an engaging rascal and should be sorry to see you fall into a pattern card of respectability. Which, I collect, is Cora's intention."

"But not, I think, mine," Eastcott answered coolly.

Lady Jersey only laughed and shook her head at him. "Fetch me a glass of champagne, Harry. Then I really do want to hear the latest *on-dits*. I don't know how it is, but you always seem to know things in advance of the rest of us!"

"Perhaps because I so often figure in the tales!" he countered. Then, with a bow, he went off to procure the champagne.

To be honest, Lord Eastcott was not in the least distressed that Sally Jersey had drawn him away from Felicity. Though he distinctly disliked horses, Eastcott was well aware of the maxim that one ought to keep a light hand on the reins. It would not have disturbed him to know that each of the other six gentlemen with Felicity had also vowed their willingness to show her the sights of London. *He* intended to be first. Meanwhile, let the girl have the heady sensation of knowing herself a success and she would feel all the less constraint when she next found herself in his company.

Lady Carrington and her daughter, on the other hand, were not at all pleased at Felicity's success. Indeed, it was early when a petulant Lucinda pleaded the headache and persuaded her mother to call for their carriage. Lady Carrington was not unwilling. Lucinda was a headstrong girl whom she found it difficult to check, and she recognised danger in the way Lucinda's eyes now glittered. Once in the carriage, Lady Carrington shook her head decisively. "You shall have to take care, Lucinda. Miss Lyford is definitely a danger to us. We can't trust Sir Anthony and Lord Eastcott not to develop a *tendre* for the girl. And everyone, you know, is expecting one or t'other—Sir Anthony, I hope—to come up to scratch this Season. If they don't, Cora Meecham won't be the only one to say you're on the shelf. And, indeed, I must say that it's an odd thing a girl with your looks is still unspoken for!"

Nettled, Lucinda retorted, "You were the one who said that Harcourt and Charleton wouldn't do! *You* said I ought to look higher! And if Papa could only contrive something more handsome in the way of a settlement, I would have a far better chance!"

"You *should* know, if you do not, that it costs a great deal to live in London and keep a household and dress a girl for the Season. Your Papa, moreover, has had the worst luck lately with his ventures. One can only console oneself with the reflection that if your portion is modest, Miss Lyford must be virtually penniless. Geoffrey Lyford was a shockingly loose screw who left nothing but debts! So do give over your pouting, Lucinda. The situation only wants resolution! Recollect that it took me three full Seasons to coax your father into declaring himself, and I was considered at least as handsome as you, in my salad days."

The situation was not, however, quite so simple as either lady envisioned. It was neither Miss Carrington's modest dowry nor her mother's high ambitions alone that had, thus far, defeated them. Lucinda was indeed beautiful but, as was swiftly borne in on her suitors, she was all too aware of this fact and no gentleman was ever so deceived as to suppose she cared one whit what problems *he* might have. Lady Carrington only made matters worse for, placed side by side with her daughter, no gentleman could doubt that here was Lucinda's future. Still, beauty might have carried the day had unfortunate circumstances not forced Lucinda to retire from London at the height of the Season, two years in a row. The first time was due to a case of the measles contracted from Lucinda's abigail who had, in turn, contracted her case from her young nephew, who was five. The second circumstance was her father's speculation on a very private, very risky venture which had failed. Naturally it had been impossible to admit the truth and both times it had been given out that Miss Lucinda was exhausted by the exigencies of the Season and had retired to the country to rest. Unfortunately, it was generally held, among the ton, that Lucinda had withdrawn out of caprice. Certainly she was believed to be of a temperament to do so. Thus it was that Woodhall and Eastcott were two of the very few who still seemed seriously to aspire to her hand. And even they had bluntly admitted they considered Lucinda heartless. At three and twenty, Lucinda might not yet be desperate, but she was beginning to feel that if these two failed her, she must soon become so. Not that either was an ideal suitor. Cora Meecham's will was a risky thing on which to base the hope that Lord Eastcott might bring himself about again. As for Woodhall, he was, to be sure, sufficiently a man of the ton to bring one the most elegant of trifles, but he never pretended to believe one's prettiest speeches. And although he was frequently to be seen at Almack's and the most exclusive of ton parties, he was equally likely to be found at Gentleman Jackson's Boxing Saloon or drinking Blue Ruin at Cribb's Parlour. He drove to an inch and had the most exquisite of matched chestnuts. But not once, in all the times he had taken Miss Lucinda Carrington driving, had he offered to lend her the reins even

though he must have known how much it would add
to her consequence to be seen tooling his curricle
about the park. Miss Carrington was, however,
willing to overlook all of these faults, secure in the
conviction that he would improve once he was leg-
shackled. To be sure, Lord Eastcott would be a more
delightful companion, but Lucinda had only to contemplate herself as mistress of Woodhall Manor, Sir
Anthony's townhouse, and his fortune, coupled with
Lady Meecham's, to know she was right to continue
in her determination to bring Sir Anthony up to
scratch and to marry him . . . *before* Lord Eastcott
found a wife.

Lucinda Carrington would have been surprised to
know that Sir Anthony was well aware of her
thoughts. Since he felt himself equal, however, to
dealing with any female, he was not unduly concerned. As to whether Sir Anthony intended to propose to Lucinda, that was a question he was not yet
prepared to answer. When Aunt Cora had said that
she felt Lucinda to be heartless, he had answered
quite truthfully that he felt the fact only argued that
he and Miss Carrington were well suited. Sir Anthony
genuinely believed himself to be a cold man and
therefore unlikely ever to lose his heart to any
woman. It might, then, be sensible to betrothe himself
to a female who was of equally cold temperament
and thus unlikely to expect of him a degree of
warmth he would be unable to give her. And yet, Sir
Anthony found himself strangely reluctant to come to
the point of speaking to Lucinda's father. He consoled
himself with the knowledge that there was yet plenty
of time. Miss Lucinda Carrington was, in any case,
more likely to prove a dutiful wife if she were not

quite so sure of her hold on Sir Anthony. But the final, if somewhat irrelevant, consideration was that all of London appeared to expect the betrothal and Sir Anthony was not the man to enjoy having his hand forced. Therefore, he waited.

Long after Miss Lucinda Carrington sought her bed, Felicity and her hostess said good night to the last of the departing guests. Lady Meecham was inclined to pronounce the party a success. "Depend upon it!" she said with delight. "You will be welcome everywhere! I am most pleased, my dear, most pleased. And I shall be surprised if we do not soon have in hand the vouchers for Almack's!"

Felicity was too tired to do more than smile, a circumstance that caused Lady Meecham to send her immediately up to bed. Felicity was only too happy to obey.

Upstairs, Annie waited to help Felicity undress and to hear the report of her young mistress's triumph. She listened in silence, then said with well-concealed pride, "I won't say that I'm not pleased, Miss Felicity, for I am, but I hope I won't find this turning your head! You've come to London to find a husband, not to turn into a giddy puss of a girl."

Felicity, however, knew her abigail too well to be deceived. With a tired smile she quizzed her. "Oh, but I want to be giddy, Annie! It seems forever since I've had any opportunity to be other than unhappy!"

Her back to Felicity, Annie's face softened as she said quietly, "Aye, Miss Felicity, I know it has. All I ask is that you hold onto enough of your common sense so that you're not taken in by some honey-tongued betrayer!"

Impulsively, Felicity hugged her abigail as she said, "How can I be, with you to protect me, Annie?"

"Give over your nonsense, now do, Miss Felicity!" Annie said as she pulled away. "Remember what's proper!"

"I'll try, Annie," Felicity answered, more than a hint of laughter in her eyes.

With that, Annie had to be satisfied and she admonished Felicity to try and go to sleep for gentlemen didn't like to see ladies with circles under their eyes. Demurely, Felicity climbed into bed under her abigail's gaze. Annie then blew out the last of the candles and withdrew to her own tiny quarters, at the top of the house, to worry, once more, about her young mistress. Felicity herself lay awake a little longer, lost in the pleasantest of daydreams.

VII

Upon his return to London a few days later, Sir Anthony Woodhall was not surprised to find Miss Lyford's name on several tongues. Aunt Cora's party had been certain to trigger interest in her guest. Indeed, the sight of Felicity would be enough to convince any number of susceptible young men that they were enamoured of her. Nevertheless, when he called at his aunt's house, he found it difficult to suppress a shudder of distaste at the sight of so many callow youths assembled at one time. Harry was there, of course, but so was Mr. Philip Crofton. The latter made Woodhall smile and he wondered if Miss Lyford understood just how honoured she ought to feel, for Crofton had never before been known to show an interest in any young lady of the ton. As for Harry, to be sure he appeared to be flirting with Aunt Cora, *not* Miss Lyford, but Sir Anthony was not deceived. It was therefore somewhat irritably that he greeted Lady Meecham. "Hallo, Aunt Cora. Must you encourage all these puppies to hang about?"

"Jealous?" she retorted.

"Not a bit of it! My sensibilities are merely offended."

Lord Eastcott rose to his feet as he said lazily, "I should scarcely call myself a puppy, Tony."

"No, you're even worse!" Sir Anthony retorted unsympathetically.

At that moment, Felicity, who had been deep in conversation with one of her admirers, looked up and saw Woodhall. Immediately she called out to him, "Sir Anthony! You missed my party; it was such fun!"

With a bored smile he replied, "Was it, child? How nice."

Flattened by his unexpected hauteur, Felicity turned her head away from Sir Anthony and stiffly addressed some remark to Mr. Crofton, who was delighted with the attention. Aware of Felicity's dismay, Sir Anthony was annoyed with himself for being so abrupt with her. His temper was further exacerbated by Eastcott, who said in his habitual lazy voice, "Now Tony, was that kind of you? I believe you've quite spoiled her pleasure at seeing you again. Now I . . . I should never bo so cow-handed with a female, only with my horses."

"I wish you will go away, Harry!" Sir Anthony told him impatiently.

"No doubt," Eastcott agreed sympathetically. "How unfortunate that I have no intention of fulfilling your wish. I find the sight of Miss Lyford too, er, captivating, shall we say? Don't you?"

"No, I don't!" Woodhall retorted. "I haven't the slightest interest in Miss Lyford or her beaux!"

"How fortunate," Eastcott murmured, "since I am persuaded the feelings are quite mutual."

This was too much for Sir Anthony and, goaded, he

turned to Lady Meecham. "I see, Aunt Cora, that you are engaged and I shall return another time to visit with you."

"But no!" Eastcott protested. "Aunt Cora will surely excuse me and I, well noted for my exquisite tact, will happily withdraw so that you may have a comfortable cose together. No, don't bother to thank me, Tony! I am delighted to be of service."

So saying, Lord Eastcott strolled over to join the group around Felicity. Sir Anthony watched him, a distinct urge in his breast to kick rather than thank his cousin. Lady Meecham's tart voice brought his attention back to her. "Well, nephew, do you intend to stand all day? You know I can't abide looking up at people!"

Hastily, Woodhall seated himself. "I'm sorry, Aunt Cora." Then, irritably, he added, "Must you encourage Harry to dangle after her, ma'am? You must know it is not the thing."

Lady Meecham looked at Sir Anthony with a hauteur that would have daunted anyone less well acquainted with her. "Really, Anthony, I cannot conceive what concern it is of *yours* who, as you so crudely put it, dangles after Miss Lyford! As for Harold, why not? She is looking for a husband and he requires a wife. What could be more suitable? In any event," she added hastily as she saw that he was about to tell her, "you must know very well that Harold requires no encouragement. To the contrary, I should have supposed he thrives on opposition. Or are you worried about my will, Anthony?"

Woodhall glared at Lady Meecham. "I was *not* thinking about that, Aunt Cora. I was thinking of Miss Lyford."

Lady Meecham studied his face a moment, then shrugged. "Oh, well, if that is all! You may leave Miss Lyford's welfare to me. Tell me, instead, how did you find Woodhall Manor?"

Sir Anthony was obliged to suppress the other observations he had been about to make and talk about his trip. Meanwhile, the group around Felicity began reluctantly to disperse. Lord Eastcott, who indeed prided himself on his light touch, was among the first to depart. Mr. Philip Crofton was the last and reminded Lady Meecham of a loyal dog jealously guarding its mistress. His face had noticeably relaxed as soon as Lord Eastcott took his leave, but he could not be entirely easy until the others had gone as well. Mr. Crofton would, in fact, have preferred to stay and guard Felicity from Sir Anthony, but he was too much the gentleman to remain beyond the prescribed length of time for a morning call. Lady Meecham kept Sir Anthony's attention engaged for a few minutes after the gentlemen had left, then struggled to her feet as she said, "There's something I wanted to show you, Anthony. A letter from your cousin Letty. No, no, wait here. It won't take me above a moment to find it. Have Felicity tell you about her party."

Felicity, who had been about to escape the room, was obliged to stop and face Sir Anthony with as good a grace as she could manage. Woodhall merely frowned, torn between amusement and irritation at such an obvious attempt to throw them together. His manners, however, were too good to permit him to snub Felicity and, after Lady Meecham had gone, he said rather kindly, "Well, Miss Lyford, won't you tell me about your party?"

Sir Anthony was, she decided, being sarcastic and
with a chilly dignity that could only emphasize her
youth, Felicity said, "I am aware, sir, that it cannot
be of the slightest interest to you and I assure you,
you need not feel obliged to engage me in civil conversation."

"All right," he said agreeably, "I shan't. I'll engage
you in uncivil conversation instead." With difficulty,
Felicity suppressed a smile, but all her efforts could
not prevent a talltale quiver in her cheeks. Thus encouraged, Woodhall went on, "Would you care to
boast about your beaux? I assure you I should enjoy
it if you did."

Felicity cast him a withering glance and said,
"Well, I should not enjoy it, Sir Anthony!"

"What? Not even Mr. Crofton? You must know that
he is a most admirable conquest! Never before has
that estimable gentleman discovered a maiden who
embodied a sufficient degree of good sense, house-
wifely attributes, pleasant countenance, refinement,
and good breeding to engage his interest. Surely it
must add to your esteem to have attached such a dis-
criminating fellow?"

Felicity spoke as though to herself. "Abominable! I
wonder . . . does he hope to provoke me into saying
something unbecoming? For I daresay he has very
little regard for my maidenly reserve."

"Oh, none at all!" Sir Anthony agreed cordially. As
she cast him a fulminating look, he laughed and
strolled over to her. Then, as he possessed himself of
Felicity's hands, Sir Anthony said, "Come, Miss Lyford! Would you prefer I treated you as a Bath miss?
All simpering and fluttering shyness, without two
thoughts to rub together? Would you?" he demanded.

Felicity looked up at Sir Anthony and tried, fruitlessly, to free her hands. When she found she could not, Felicity said crossly, "Well, no, but must you be so disagreeable? I need not be a Bath miss to feel a . . . a degree of repugnance in discussing affairs of the heart."

Something in her voice made Sir Anthony release her hands and ask sharply, "What is it, Miss Lyford? Do you mean to tell me you find your affections already attached? To Crofton?" She shook her head without looking at Woodhall. He frowned as a new thought struck him and he said grimly, "I hope you do not mean to say you've a *tendre* for Lord Eastcott. He is my cousin, but I should feel myself derelict did I not warn you that he is a ramshackle fellow and will not do for you. In spite of my aunt's schemes!"

Felicity, whose colour had heightened alarmingly, now went pale. Her voice trembling slightly, she said, "How insufferable of you to try to meddle in my affairs this way, Sir Anthony! I collect you have such a high notion of your own consequence that you believe everyone must listen to what you say! Well, I need not."

Impatiently, Woodhall looked down at Felicity as he retorted, "You mistake me, Miss Lyford! I only meant to give you a friendly warning. You are new to London and cannot know my cousin's reputation! Nor is my aunt likely to tell you. But I see my words come too late, Harry has already found a place in your regard. I only hope you may not be disappointed in him! He might, as a result of Lady Meecham's will, choose to marry, but I cannot believe he will change his essential nature."

"Insufferable!" Felicity retorted in a rage. "Insufferably arrogant I should rather have said! I am grateful for your concern, my dear sir, however I do not count myself a green miss who must be guided by your no doubt infallible judgement!"

Goaded beyond endurance, Sir Anthony answered, "Green miss? Not at all! I find you a scruffy provincial chit who has no presence or breeding or sense! You haven't the least notion of how to go on, as must be obvious to everyone with eyes. I thank God I have not the responsibility of looking after you for I am certain you will find a way to cast yourself into the briars!"

Felicity curtsied and said primly, "Why, Sir Anthony, how happy I am to finally be in agreement with you on some matter! I, too, thank God you have not the responsibility of taking care of me!"

Sir Anthony most definitely tried to frown, but the frown dissolved into an outright laugh. "Abominable child!"

"I am not a child!" Felicity answered stiffly.

"No, you are a most redoubtable young lady," he said soothingly. He spoiled this encomium, however, by adding, "With more courage than sense."

"Indeed?" Felicity asked frostily. "How strange! I have it on excellent authority that you consider me to have an *excess* of common sense."

This time Sir Anthony frowned in earnest. "Did I say so? I cannot recollect. . . ."

"Miss Carrington," Felicity supplied the name gently.

Startled, Sir Anthony said, "But surely she cannot have told you so?"

Felicity merely smiled sweetly at Woodhall and waited to see what effect this news would have on him. To her disappointment, he half turned away so that she could no longer see his face. Sir Anthony did not, however, appear unduly disturbed, Felicity noted crossly.

In this she was mistaken. Sir Anthony was in fact very disturbed. That Lucinda was heartless he already knew; that she could be so vulgar was as annoying as it was unexpected. Sir Anthony was still digesting this view of Miss Carrington when his aunt returned to the room. "At dagger points again, are you?" Lady Meecham asked waspishly.

Felicity reddened and Sir Anthony favoured Cora with a slight bow. Lady Meecham drew in her breath in a gesture Sir Anthony knew well from his childhood and he suddenly felt the need to protect Miss Lyford from her anger. One glance at Miss Lyford's white face, moreover, was sufficient to inform him that she, too, recognised Lady Meecham's intent. Without thinking, Sir Anthony moved closer to Felicity and placed a hand on her shoulder. "You'd best get your cloak," he said gently, "if we're going for that drive."

Too grateful to cavil at Sir Anthony's tactics, Felicity nodded and hurried from the room, her eyes lowered to avoid looking at Lady Meecham. She, however, ignored the still pale and slightly shaky young girl. Instead, Cora eyed Woodhall speculatively. Too shrewd to ask his motives, she contented herself with discussing the letter she had gone to fetch. It was a topic that heartily bored both of them.

Fifteen minutes later, it was a very grateful and enchantingly shy girl that Sir Anthony escorted out the door. Now Sir Anthony had never been enamoured of females who had nothing to say for themselves, but

when Miss Lyford smiled up at him with glowing
eyes, it somehow seemed unimportant that she was
silent. It was only after Tifton had closed the door behind them that the spell was broken. "Sir Anthony,"
Felicity said in a puzzled voice, "I don't see any carriage."

"I know," he said wryly. "Should you mind walking,
instead? I didn't bring my carriage, you see, but it
was the only thing I could think of when Aunt Cora
started to scold us."

"Did you know, then?" Felicity asked, looking up at
him. "I wondered. I felt ready to sink, for I knew she
was angry with me."

"Is that the only reason you accepted my invitation?" Sir Anthony asked, his eyes fixed on her eyes.

Felicity found she could not bear such close scrutiny and turned her face away as she started to answer. But Sir Anthony would have none of that. He
stopped and gently took Miss Lyford's chin in his
hand and made her look at him. There was a slight
catch in Felicity's voice as she said, "Were I not such
a coward, sir, I should most certainly have declined."

Taken aback, Sir Anthony abruptly let go of her
chin and said, "*What?*"

As she turned a deep crimson, Felicity stammered,
"I meant—that is. . . ." She took a breath and her
words tumbled over one another as she tried to explain, "I know you didn't want to ask me—that you
were only being kind. And I know I ought not to
have accepted, only I can't bear it when Lady
Meecham scolds me!" Felicity saw his face darken
with displeasure and she hastened to add, "I ought
not to be ungrateful, I know, and Lady Meecham has
been so kind to me, but I cannot bear to have anyone

so angry at me. And you *did* offer to take me out of the house and it seemed——"

Abruptly he cut her short. "But you don't mind my company?" he demanded.

Startled, Felicity answered, "Why no, of course not! But I——"

Once more Sir Anthony cut her short. Rather roughly he said, "You seem uncommonly grateful for kindness!"

Tilting up her chin, Felicity answered, "Why yes, I suppose I am. But then, you see, I haven't known very much of it in my life, and I cannot bring myself to treat it lightly."

"Before your mother died——" Sir Anthony began.

"Before my mother died was certainly better than after!" Felicity retorted bitterly. "But my mother was never one to spoil her children. My father's ideas, moreover, were of paramount importance to her and *he* held girls to be of little value!" Felicity paused, uncertainly, and looked at Sir Anthony's face. It was impassive. She sighed, but went on quietly, "I should not have said that, I know. And no doubt I have shocked you. But, as you have surely noticed, I am not always capable of guarding my tongue. You can take me back now if you want. I-I'll understand."

"No, I *don't* want to take you back just yet," Sir Anthony said decisively. "But I *do* want to start walking—you look chilled."

With a smile she confessed, "I am a bit. Could we walk rather briskly?"

"Briskly it shall be!" he confirmed, with deceptive lightness.

He set himself to amuse and more than one person stopped to smile at the laughing couple who walked with such energy on such a chilly day. To his surprise, Sir Anthony found Miss Lyford remarkably well informed. When he taxed her with being a bluestocking, she merely shook her head and observed that at Lyford Park she had had ample time to read. It was very pleasant, he discovered, to have someone to share his ideas with—someone who had read the same books and enjoyed the same authors. Even more astonishing was the realisation that he preferred to have Miss Lyford state her opinions plainly as she did. Sir Anthony was unaccustomed to females who did not automatically second his views.

Eventually, of course, they found themselves back at Lady Meecham's townhouse. Sir Anthony intended to take his leave as soon as Tifton opened the door to Felicity. In this, however, he was forestalled. With a voice that bespoke doom, Tifton greeted the pair by informing Sir Anthony, "Your mother has come to call."

Whatever response Felicity expected, it was not the softly ejaculated "Damme!" she heard beside her. A moment later she was wondering if she had heard correctly, for Sir Anthony appeared totally unconcerned as he said, "Thank you, Tifton. Are they in the drawing room?"

Woodenly Tifton replied, "No, sir, they are enjoying a quiet luncheon together."

"Luncheon?" Felicity repeated in dismay. "I had no idea it was so late!"

At this Tifton permitted himself to unbend and it was almost with a smile that he said, "Well, as to that, I strongly doubt that you will find her ladyship distressed at your tardiness. Indeed, upon being informed that you still had not returned, her ladyship made some comment about pretty young ladies in their first Season. Always a good sign, if I may say so."

"You may," Sir Anthony said dryly. "You may also show us to the dining room. I've a fancy to see how my mother and my aunt are getting along."

"Most politely—so far," Tifton permitted himself to say rather cryptically, before he became once more the very correct major domo of Lady Meecham's staff. Nor did he speak again until he made the rather prim announcement, "Miss Lyford and Sir Anthony!"

Two sets of eyes immediately turned to the pair. Lady Meecham permitted herself a triumphant smile as she said, "Felicity! Anthony! Come in, children. Anthony, introduce Miss Lyford to your mother. Girl I was telling you about, Alice."

As her son dutifully presented Felicity, Alice Woodhall stared openly, no hint of welcome on her face. Indeed, it seemed to Felicity that Lady Woodhall regarded her with pronounced disfavour. In this, however, she underestimated her ladyship. Lady Woodhall had, admittedly, come prepared to dislike the girl for, secluded as she was, rumours had nonetheless reached Lady Woodhall. Rumours of a young lady staying with Cora. This combined with the knowledge of Cora's absurd will had led Lady Woodhall to the same conclusion Lord Eastcott had reached. And it was, quite naturally, intolerable that Cora should presume to interfere in Anthony's affairs. Nevertheless, confronted with Miss Lyford, Lady Woodhall found herself forced to reconsider. Fine grey eyes met hers steadily and there was an air of gentle determination about Felicity that Lady Woodhall could only admire. Yet she did not appear to thrust herself forward. Curls framed a charming face and a fashionable walking dress set off her figure to advantage, but the girl clearly eschewed the excesses of the current fashion season, unlike certain other young ladies that Lady Woodhall was aware of. Aye, that was the problem. Alice might resent her sister's interference, but there was no denying that Lady Woodhall disliked Miss Carrington even more. One would not, of course, wish Anthony to regard Cora's vulgar scheme, but if the girl succeeded in distracting him, however briefly, from the Carrington chit, a mother must be grateful. It was thus that Lady Woodhall surprised everyone, including herself, by saying graciously, "Hello, Miss Lyford. I hope you are enjoying your Season as much as I did mine?"

"Oh, yes!" Felicity answered warmly. "How could I not, when Lady Meecham has been so kind to me?"

"Stuff!" Cora snorted, not at all displeased. "I always wondered what it would be like to launch a daughter, and now I know. A delight! I consider it to have been most selfish of you, Alice, not to allow me to share in presenting your girls."

Lady Woodhall's lips compressed into a thin line as she recalled her sister loudly proclaiming—at the time—that she had no intention of curtailing her own amusements to play nursemaid to schoolroom misses. Sir Anthony spoke hastily as he recognised the martial light in his mother's eyes, "Confess, Aunt Cora! You would not think it half so much fun were Miss Lyford a mere niece."

Lady Meecham chose to smile, but her voice was a trifle sharp as she commanded, "Well, don't stand there, the pair of you—sit down!"

Quickly, Felicity took her accustomed place at the

table and Anthony followed meekly. It did not pass unnoticed that he chose the chair next to Felicity's, but none of the ladies were disposed to object. Indeed, with unspoken consent, Cora and Alice resumed their discussion about the Royal Family. One might have been pardoned for assuming that this must be a safe topic but, in point of fact, it was not and the two sisters were soon embroiled in a spirited argument. Felicity, left to Sir Anthony's company, suddenly found herself unaccountably shy. Aware of her shyness but misguessing its cause, Woodhall said quietly, "It don't signify, you know, for they are both quite enjoying themselves!"

"Are they?" she answered dubiously.

He nodded. "Give you my word. It keeps them feeling young, I'd wager. In any event, I cannot recollect any occasion on which they have met without all but coming to blows—usually over the least sort of excuse." In spite of herself, Felicity laughed softly and Sir Anthony said, "That's better! I begin to believe Crofton did not exaggerate when he said that you would take the ton by storm, Miss Lyford!"

Felicity smiled but shook her head, a marked degree of restraint in her voice as she said, "I think not, Sir Anthony. Recollect my circumstances! I *am* virtually penniless, you know."

"A man who ignores you for such a reason as that must either be a fool or desperate." Seeing that she merely greeted his words with a sceptical shake of her head, Sir Anthony rallied Felicity. "Come, Miss Lyford! You would surely not be so uncivil as to contradict me?"

Felicity smiled but could not bring herself to laugh.

"I can only say that you are naive, sir, if you think it will not make a difference."

Sir Anthony was well aware of the justice of Felicity's remark. It struck him, however, as remarkably ill-bred of her to put what they both knew into words; Lucinda would never have done so. At least, not to him. It was therefore with a touch of asperity that Woodhall said, "Ought you to speak so frankly to me, Miss Lyford?"

To his surprise, Felicity met Woodhall's quelling stare with a smile of amusement. "Of course not," she replied, with a tiny sigh. "And yet, do you know, I cannot bring myself to believe that you would not understand. Or that you would betray what I told you in confidence."

"What? A compliment?" Sir Anthony quizzed her. "Are you feeling well, Miss Lyford?"

"Now you are roasting me!" Felicity retorted coolly. "I hope I may be able to acknowledge your good qualities as well as your faults."

"Now, now," Sir Anthony admonished her. "You ought not to refer to a gentleman's faults—if you wish to find a husband—except to say that he has none!"

Nettled, Felicity said, "I should be a remarkably green girl to ignore either. Indeed, I have always thought that if one were considering matrimony one ought to have as few illusions as possible about the person one was about to marry! What is the use of discovering after marriage that one's spouse has habits one cannot abide? If one knows beforehand one can either cry off or accustom oneself, in advance, to the inevitable."

"I see," Woodhall said with heavy irony, "and what faults ought *your* future husband to be apprised of?"

Felicity shrugged and answered evenly, "My circumstances. My temper." She paused and her eyes began to dance. With a laugh, she said, "And, of course, my wretched tongue!"

In spite of himself, Sir Anthony laughed also. "Serious sins, indeed." Then, seeing the speculative look in her eyes, he said, "No, Miss Lyford, I have no intention of being equally frank about *my* shortcomings."

"Fainthearted?" Felicity shot back.

"Inevitably!" he retorted. "Consider! I have the handicap of having lived several years longer than you and hence the opportunity to have developed more faults. Not," he added, holding up a hand, "that I should be so foolish as to claim that at your age I was a paragon of virtue."

"Just as well," Felicity said outrageously, "for I should never have swallowed such a plumper."

"Raked me over the coals, would you have?"

Drawing herself up with dignity, Felicity said, "To use your words, Sir Anthony, I should not dream of being so uncivil."

Once more he laughed, this time drawing Lady Meecham's attention. Tartly, she demanded, "I hope you are enjoying yourselves, Anthony? No doubt it is far too much to expect that you would devote any part of your attention to your mother or myself!"

Not in the least perturbed by his aunt's ill-humour, Sir Anthony replied easily, "I thought you wished me to be polite to Miss Lyford."

Lady Meecham was mollified but nevertheless sniffed, "You needn't think it will be so easy to fix your interest with the girl. Harry can be most charming!"

Embarrassed at this frank discussion of her circumstances, Felicity blushed furiously. Particularly as Lady Woodhall entered the fray. "Harry? That *wastrel*? I wonder you can mention his name in the same breath as Anthony's! Or that you even care to expose a young girl such as Miss Lyford to his company. Indeed——"

"Indeed, Mother, it is time we were going!" Sir Anthony said, cutting her short ruthlessly.

For a moment, Lady Woodhall glared at her son. Then she straightened her shoulders and said stiffly, "I feel one of my spasms coming on."

Sir Anthony's face softened as he said, "Are you really unwell, Mother? In that event I must certainly take you home."

She nodded and there was nothing for it but for everyone to rise from the table. Genuine concern was evident on Sir Anthony's face as he gave his mother his arm to lean on. And, indeed, it quickly became clear, even to Felicity, that Lady Woodhall was in true distress. Lady Meecham went so far as to suggest that her sister lie down in the drawing room and her own doctor be fetched. This, Alice Woodhall declined, stating that once an attack had begun, the best thing was for her to take to her *own* bed and remain there for several days. In any event, Maria would know just what to do for her and everyone would be more comfortable. At these sensible words, Cora abandoned the attempt to persuade her sister to stay and contented herself with seeing that Alice was as comfortable as possible in her carriage. When she returned to the drawing, room, where Felicity was waiting, Lady Meecham looked older than her years. Rather sharply, she told the girl, "You needn't look like that! I *am* fond of my sister. And she *is* ill."

There was a pause and Cora went on, with some satisfaction, "Came to look you over, Felicity. Seemed to like you." For a moment, it was evident that pleasant fantasies occupied Lady Meecham's mind. Then with a sigh, she said, "Ah, well, we needn't expect anything to come of Alice's visit, for very likely nothing will!"

For once, Lady Meecham was quite wrong.

VIII

When word of Lady Alice Woodhall's call on Miss
Felicity Lyford leaked out, as it inevitably did, the
ton was disposed to be even kinder to Felicity than
had already been the case. And, indeed, it was not
surprising. Felicity was acknowledged to be a very
prettily behaved young girl and, in view of Lady
Meecham's plans for the girl, not the most matchmak-
ing of mamas could object to her cherished daughter
being seen in company with Miss Lyford. For if her
presence drew the dangerous Lord Harold Eastcott,
he was soon seen to be interested only in Felicity.
And as not the most optimistic of mothers (aside from
Lady Carrington) felt there was any hope of bringing
Sir Anthony to the point of offering for her daughter,
his interest in Felicity merely prompted the rather
malicious hope that Lucinda Carrington would find
herself taken down a peg or two. So when the rumour
circulated that Lady Woodhall had met and been
pleased to approve of Miss Lyford, the already plenti-
ful invitations increased. Even the coveted vouchers
for Almack's arrived in time for the first subscription
ball of the Season to be given there. Only the Car-

ringtons stood aloof from the general approval accorded Lady Meecham's protégée, and this was scarcely a circumstance which weighed heavily on her shoulders.

It would have taken a great deal, in fact, to have dampened Felicity's spirits. For the first time in her life, she met with genuine kindness everywhere she went. If most of the gentlemen who flirted with her were not in earnest, nevertheless their admiration was. Moreover, amid the whirl of balls, routs, breakfasts, and shopping expeditions, Felicity began to blossom and even Annie lost her habitual scowl as she watched her young mistress enjoying herself so thoroughly as the days passed.

Inevitably, the ton began to take an intense interest in which cousin would end up leg-shackled to Miss Lyford. Lord Harry was noted to be assiduous in his attentions, but it could not be denied that Sir Anthony was seeing rather less of Miss Carrington of late. As for Felicity, if her eyes followed Sir Anthony perhaps more than they ought to have, it was done so discreetly that most observers gave it as their opinion that she preferred Lord Harry. She laughed easily in his company, and if she was too well-bred to hang on his sleeve, neither did she frown at him as she was distinctly seen to have done with Sir Anthony. Nor would Sir Anthony or Lord Eastcott have disagreed with this assessment. Indeed, Harry began to ask himself if perhaps it was not time to declare himself. One did not wish to startle the girl, but neither did one wish to take the risk that Tony would precede one in marriage. In the end, he decided to test the waters by taking Felicity to meet his mother. Surely that would apprise Miss Lyford of his intentions and Harry could study her reaction.

In this Harry had underestimated Felicity's naiveté. She was unaware of most of the gossip concerning Lady Eastcott and she had no notion how unusual such a visit might be. Certainly her brother Richard's wife, Sally, had been a frequent visitor to Lyford Park well before an engagement had even been considered. So the arrangements were made and, on a sunny spring morning, Felicity and Lord Eastcott set out for the small estate that was Lady Eastcott's current residence.

It was a charming place, not far from London, and at her first sight of it, Felicity exclaimed, "How pretty! Has it been in your family long?"

As the carriage turned up the long drive, Lord Eastcott coughed and said, "Er, no. That is, it don't belong to my mother. She's a guest of—of Mr. Matthews, at the moment."

To his relief, Felicity asked no further questions, but was content to exclaim over the peacocks she saw strutting on a terrace. The birds did not seem particularly pleased to be there, but there was no question that they lent an air of the unusual to the scene. This impression was reinforced, a few minutes later, when Felicity and Harry were shown into the Red Saloon. That remarkable room included several couches of design ranging from solid English to the Egyptian, any number of tables and flower stands, also of mixed parentage, and Belgian carpets that warred with the cherry-red striped drapes. For a moment, the enormity of the room stunned Miss Lyford, but her trance was broken by a rich, throaty chuckle. "Dreadful, isn't it?" the woman said, guessing Felicity's thoughts. "But

Mr. Matthews very much enjoys the room. *I* am Lady Theresa Eastcott, Harry's mother."

Felicity blinked and focussed her eyes on the tall, slender woman who was holding out a hand to her. Automatically, Felicity took it. Lady Eastcott's lovely auburn curls, dressed high on her head, quivered as she laughed again. "What's wrong?" she asked. "Am I not what you expected?"

"You're too young!" Felicity blurted out. Then, hastily, she added, "I mean——"

"Don't!" Lady Eastcott commanded, holding up a hand imperatively. "*Never* apologise for complimenting another woman! If you persist, I shall find myself counting years and that would be too dreadful. Instead, sit down beside me, Miss Lyford, and tell me how you find London. Harold, sit on the other side of the room and be quiet. Or you might go and wander about the grounds for a while, if you wish."

Lord Harry bowed with exquisite politeness. "I think I should prefer to stay."

"Afraid I shan't be discreet?" she asked mockingly.

Harry merely shrugged. Embarrassed by the exchange, Felicity pretended to be studying the room again. Once more Lady Eastcott's voice intruded. "If you find this astonishing, you ought to see the bright pink carriage Mr. Matthews has provided for my use. *Not* that *I* object," she added scrupulously. "It has never been a part of my character to wish to pass unnoticed and I rather enjoy the attention it draws. But come, sit beside me and tell me about yourself, Miss Lyford."

Good manners compelled Felicity to do so, but to her surprise, she soon found herself genuinely attracted to Harry's mother. It didn't matter that the lady was indeed outrageous. Perhaps that was even a part of her charm. To one bred to all the rules of polite society, Lady Eastcott could not but seem an appealing view of the alternatives. For her part, Theresa was agreeably pleased with what she saw. This was no milk-and-water chit to bore her son in a fortnight. Miss Lyford had spirit and yet the common sense that Tess herself lacked but would wish to see in her son's wife. For Tess was well aware that although her life might appear exciting and attractive to a young girl like Felicity, she had, by a lack of the ability to be prudent, denied herself much that she had once wished for. Harry looked to follow her footsteps and Theresa could only be pleased that Miss Lyford seemed to be the sort of girl who might check his excesses without caging him too close. Abruptly Lady Eastcott realised that Felicity was regarding her oddly. With twinkling eyes, she said, "You must forgive me, Miss Lyford, for I was thinking, you see, that *you* are not in the least what *I* expected!"

"Ma'am?" Felicity said blankly, rather taken aback.

Theresa hesitated, well aware that Harry would deplore such plain-spokeness, then plunged on nevertheless. "I never looked for such sense in Coral Yes, yes, I know all about her plans and *you* needn't blush, for I cannot see that you are at fault. I shan't ask whether or not you plan to have my son, for that is his affair and he has yet to require my assistance in such matters. I shall merely comment that it is far more amusing to be a matron than a young girl hampered by chaperones."

"So I have always thought," Felicity retorted, "provided one chooses one's husband with reasonable care. I have had the opportunity, you see, to consider the question before."

"What an odd girl you are," Lady Eastcott said, her eyes narrowed slightly. "But then your father was even more so. How fortunate that you need not deal with the handicap of his presence in London during your comeout. Though I daresay you won't see it that way. Daughters rarely do." Felicity chose not to answer. Instead of being offended, however, Lady Eastcott only smiled and nodded approval. "Good girl! So you're capable of holding your tongue. Admirable! Harry," she said, turning to observe her son, "you may now join us."

Lazily, without the least suggestion of impatience in his manner, Lord Eastcott rose and crossed the short distance to the couch where his mother and Felicity were seated. With continued leisure, he took the chair she indicated and negligently crossed one leg over the other. He then favoured the two ladies with his dazzling smile and said, "I am at your command, Mama."

Her eyes twinkling, Lady Eastcott replied, "Well, you might tell me the latest crim. con. stories! You must know Mr. Matthews does not precisely care for society and, at the moment, I am not in the way of hearing gossip."

Harry obliged and Felicity, listening, thought that it was one of the nice things about Lord Eastcott that he always gave one his complete attention. Nor was he likely to contradict one or make one feel a schoolroom child or tell one that one was not yet up to snuff. (Unlike a certain cousin of his!) To one who had grown up accustomed to either being considered of no consequence and therefore ignored, or else shouted at by her irrascible father, this was pleasant treatment indeed. When Felicity was with Lord Eastcott, she found that every attention was paid to her comfort and preferences.

These were not conscious thoughts, however. Felicity was only aware that Lord Harry was quite the most handsome man she had ever seen, and one of the nicest. She was hard put, therefore, to understand why she didn't like him better. It was not, she told herself, that she was so missish as to be shocked by the scandalous stories Lord Harry was repeating to his mother. Particularly as it was evident that that redoubtable woman was hugely entertained. Both Lady Eastcott and her son, in fact, were so engrossed in the implications of a certain royal liaison that, for a moment, they were unaware that someone had entered the room. Lady Eastcott was the first to recover. "Mr. Matthews!" she cried, rising to her feet and crossing the room to greet him.

Felicity stared at the newcomer with interest. Mr. Matthews was a tall, stoutly built gentleman whom one would at once have pegged as having more amiability than breeding. Nor was this impression contradicted when he enveloped Lady Eastcott in a generous hug and kissed her cheek soundly. As Mr. Matthews became aware of Felicity's fascinated gaze and Lord Harry's stunned countenance, the gentleman chuckled. Mr. Matthews released Lady Eastcott and said, "So this is your son, Tess. Well, well, it seems quite impossible to me, you know, that you could have such a full-grown lad." He studied Harry for a moment, then said frankly, "I've no doubt you're wishing me at Jericho, but your mama is a grown woman and I'm very fond of her."

But the words were unnecessary. Harry's good manners had already reasserted themselves and he said, with a creditable smile, "On the contrary! I only hope you may have no objection to my trespassing on your property. The house is a very beautiful one."

Astonished and gratified by this unlooked for acceptance, Mr. Matthews seemed to glow with pleasure. Then his genial eyes caught sight of Felicity and he said, "Well, and who is the lovely young lady?"

With scarcely a pause, Harry said smoothly, "Miss Lyford, may I present Mr. Matthews? Mr. Matthews, Miss Felicity Lyford."

Felicity would have curtsied, but instead found one of her hands engulfed in Mr. Matthews' large ones. He looked down at her with a distinct twinkle in his eyes as he said, "You needn't be frightened of me, you know! I'm really the gentlest of fellows."

Suddenly Felicity smiled, a hint of mischief in her eyes as she replied, "I don't think I would say I was *frightened* so much as fascinated. You seem a most unusual person."

Mr. Matthews cocked his head. "Now I wonder. Is that a polite way of saying I'm vulgar? I am, you know. There's them that say I have more money than manners. And I haven't the patience for tittle-tattle! Rather be finding out about things. And I do, you know. I can tell you about clocks and iron works and steam engines and I'm even up on politics. Or take travel. I've been to every country on the continent and even visited the Americas. Didn't waste my time, either! I can tell you how they live and work and enjoy themselves and even what sort of talking will most likely start a fight. But there's no denying I'd be out of place in the Queen's Drawing Room. *Not* that I'd ever think of such a thing as presenting myself *there!*"

He paused for breath and Lady Eastcott said, her chin tilted up belligerently, "*I* could think of it! But I won't, for I know how much you would dislike it, Mr. Matthews." She turned to Felicity and said, "Well, Miss Lyford? You weren't intended to meet Mr. Matthews, but now that you have, will you tell me what you think of him?"

Felicity was well aware what her mother, Lady Meecham, and most of the ton would unhesitatingly have replied. But even had she wished to, it would have been impossible to snub this huge, gentle person when he looked at her with such covertly anxious eyes. "I like him very well," Felicity answered firmly. She saw that Lord Eastcott looked cynical and she added, a trifle defiantly, "Indeed, I must envy anyone who has seen so much of the world."

"Kept close to home, were you?" Mr. Matthews hazarded shrewdly. "No doubt a comfort to your parents, eh, lass?"

Conscious of her colour rising, Felicity answered with a good deal of restraint, "I should not have said so, sir. It was simply a disinclination to travel on the part of my mother, and a disinclination to be burdened with his family, when he did so, on the part of my father."

Felicity broke off, aware that Lord Eastcott was suddenly at her side. As she looked up at him uncertainly, he cupped her chin in his hand and looked down at her with a lazy, mischievous smile. Carelessly he said, "Marry me and I promise you we'll see more of the world than even Mr. Matthews. We shall be gypsies, if you like, travelling about with never a care for where we go next! Shall we do it, Miss Lyford?"

Felicity smiled and said lightly, "A tempting offer, Lord Eastcott! One I shall most certainly consider."

Without haste, Harry released her chin and chuckled. "By which I collect you don't think I mean it," he said. "Well, I do, but never mind. I shall ask you again under more, er, suitable circumstances."

"I should think so!" Lady Eastcott observed indignantly.

"Eh, what's this? Serious about being leg-shackled, are you?" Mr. Matthews asked with sharp amiability. "Can't say as I blame you, my boy, with the filly such a pretty one. Tie the knot and I'll come down handsome with a wedding present!"

A look of distaste crossed Lord Harry's face and his mother hastened to intervene. "Yes, well, never mind that now, Mr. Matthews. Harry, why don't you take Miss Lyford for a turn about the gardens?"

"Aye, that's the ticket," Mr. Matthews said genially. "The best gardens in the county, they are! Ought to be, what with all they've cost me, first penny to last. But there, I don't mind sporting my blunt so long as I get value for my money. You look at the gardens and tell me what you think. And if the mood strikes you, well you won't be the first to think 'em romantic!"

With a cool bow and rigidly suppressed temper, Lord Eastcott led Felicity outside. She, on the other hand, was suppressing a gurgle of laughter that escaped as soon as the doors were shut behind them. "What a funny one!" she said in answer to Harry's look of surprise. "But I like him. And your mother."

Lord Eastcott forced himself to relax and resume

his usual languid manner. "Do you? I'm glad. I, on the other hand, shall reassure *you* by promising not to renew my offer just yet. Even if the gardens prove *very*, shall we say, romantic?" There was another gurgle of laughter and, encouraged, Harry went on, "Now let me see. I think I shall tell you about the flowers."

What Lord Eastcott lacked in knowledge, he more than made up for with a fertile, amusing inventiveness. Indeed, he was so successful in charming Felicity, that the pair were in perfect charity with one another when he returned her to Lady Meecham's townhouse late that afternoon. Even Tifton was moved to observe to the housekeeper that his lordship's suit seemed to be prospering nicely, very nicely indeed!

IX

It was several afternoons later that Felicity stood poised at the head of the staircase, debating whether or not to go for a walk. As was her custom, Lady Meecham had retired to her room for a nap, in anticipation of the evening's exertions. As she stood there, the knocker on the front door sounded and Felicity was as startled as Tifton. Few people would venture to call on the household at a time when it was generally known Lady Meecham would not be at home to visitors. Indeed, Tifton held himself in his most rigidly proper way, prepared to make clear the caller's lack of discretion. He had barely opened the door, however, when Lady Meecham's young houseguest came dashing down the stairs, as it were, crying, "Richard! Neil!"

One of the young gentlemen caught Felicity in his arms and whirled her about while the other pursed his lips in an expression quite as disapproving as Tifton's own. The young gentleman holding Miss Lyford let go of her and, at the sight of Tifton's outraged face, laughed. "Uh, oh, Fay! We're in the suds, I think." To Tifton, he said gravely, "I ought to explain that I am Miss Lyford's brother, Captain Neil Lyford, and this is Richard Lyford, her eldest brother."

As Tifton bowed coldly, Richard spoke rather sternly. "Felicity! Is this how you comport yourself? I was afraid that London——"

"Oh take a damper!" Neil said in exasperation. "Of course Fay don't act like this all the time."

Her voice carefully demure, Felicity said firmly, "In any event, we most certainly cannot discuss the matter here. I am surprised, Richard, to see *you* show so little discretion!" Then, to Tifton, she said, "I shall take them upstairs, Tifton. If her ladyship should want me, we will be in the drawing room."

It was clear from the fellow's expression that Lady Meecham was likely to be appraised of the fact even if she did not ask. Well, that could not be helped, and Felicity did not, after all, very much care.

Upstairs, Captain Lyford barely spared a glance for the elegance of the room. Instead, he took Felicity's hands in his and said, "How do you go on, Fay? Richard has told me your position."

Felicity found she could not meet her brother's eyes. Pulling her hands free, she said, "Oh, well enough, Neil. Lady Meecham is very kind to me and I have the entrée everywhere."

Richard spoke from where he stood by the window. "Your position cannot be a comfortable one, Felicity, so long as you are dependent on a stranger for all your needs and wants. And I do not even speak of the question of your dowry. I still believe you ought to come and live with Sally and me."

Felicity hesitated before she replied with a sigh, "I do not doubt the propriety of what you say, Richard."

"Then you'll return with me?" he demanded.

Resolutely she shook her head. "I cannot. Improper or not, this is the choice I have made and I will hold to it."

Richard would have protested further, but Neil cut in roughly, "Give over, Richard! I don't like Fay's position any more than you do, but it ain't her fault Father was such a loose screw as to leave her unprovided for! And don't go preaching propriety at me. I'd a damned sight sooner see Fay *happy* than *proper*."

"You think the two incompatible?" Richard asked stiffly.

"In this case I do," Neil retorted. "You can't gammon me into believing Fay would be happier lost in the countryside, dwindling into an old maid. And you're a gudgeon if you think that isn't what would happen."

"There are eligible men in my parish," Richard answered coldly.

"True enough," Neil agreed cordially. "Why, there's the squire's son, a year younger than Fay, and any number of widowers, I daresay, at least twice her age. Or were you thinking of marrying her off to the son of one of your local yeomen perhaps?"

In spite of himself, Richard laughed. "Well, no," he conceded. "All right, I promise not to preach at you any more. Today at any rate."

"He's wary of arguing with females, of late," Neil told Felicity with a wink. "Sally's breeding, you know."

Delighted, Felicity turned to her oldest brother for confirmation. His expression was answer enough and she exclaimed, "How marvelous, Richard! How is

Sally feeling? I wonder you care to leave her at such a time!"

With a rueful grin, Richard answered, "Sally's a bit ill these days, but she'll soon come about, I'm told. As for leaving her, I had no choice! Sally's mama has come for a visit and it is *she* who advised me to come to London."

"And Richard obediently agreed," Neil added promptly.

Felicity, who had met the redoubtable lady in question, had no difficulty in understanding why. She managed to suppress a smile, but her voice was a trifle unsteady as she said, "I am surprised, Richard, that you do not appeal to my sense of duty to go to Sally's side to support her through the months ahead."

Before Richard could compose a tactful reply, Neil said cheerfully, "Oh, lord, what a dust-up *that* would cause! I know he told you, just now, that he wanted you to go back with him, but I'm not quite sure what our brother would have done if you had agreed. What with Sally's mama announcing before we left that the rectory would be no place for a single young girl when Sally was lying-in!"

Richard flushed but did not contradict Neil, save to say, "I hope I am master in my own home."

"Indeed? And is the matter in question?" As three startled faces turned to see her, Lady Meecham entered the drawing room, leaning heavily on her cane. "I see Tifton was correct. You *are* entertaining, Felicity."

"Ma'am? I was sure you would not mind," Felicity said uncertainly. "May I present my brothers, Richard and Neil?"

Both gentlemen gave her their best bow. Cora

stared back intimidatingly as she said, "So I see. Well, Lyford, you don't look any more cheerful than the last time we met. And you, sir. Is it lieutenant? Captain?"

"Captain," Neil retorted cheerfully. "On leave."

"From the Peninsula?" she hazarded. At his nod, Cora went on sternly, "Well it's time and more that the matter was settled!"

"We're doing our best," Neil answered meekly.

Lady Meecham looked at him sharply, but there was no impertinence in the captain's respectful expression and she relaxed. "How long do you expect to be in London?"

"A few days," Richard answered. "At least _I_ shall be. Neil must leave to rejoin his regiment tomorrow."

"Spent most of my leave with Sally and Richard," Neil explained to his sister. "Had no notion where you were till they told me."

With a thump of her cane, Lady Meecham drew the attention back to herself. "Well then, I suppose you will want to join us this evening. My nephew is making up a party to take us to Vauxhall. Felicity has not yet been there, you know. He won't be pleased to learn you are coming, but that don't signify."

Neil cocked an eyebrow at his sister. "Shall I ask which nephew it's to be?"

Once more Lady Meecham eyed the captain sharply. "Heard about that, have you? I hope you don't mean to cut up stiff."

Mildly, Neil replied, "I? It's not my place to do so. In any event, I ain't known Fay all these years without learning she'll do as she chooses. If she wants one of your nephews, she'll have him regardless of what _we_ think. And if she don't, she won't." He paused, then said with a smile, "Fay ain't a fool. She won't marry a man who ain't right for her."

From the expression on Richard's face, it was to be inferred that he did not share this comfortable conviction. He was too much the gentleman, however, to speak his mind bluntly to Lady Meecham about her nephews. In any case, he reassured himself, *his* consent was required before Felicity could marry and he would not give it lightly. "Well?" Lady Meecham said, interrupting Richard's thoughts, "shall we settle it about tonight, then? How you'll dress and when you'll be here?"

The two gentlemen stayed only a few minutes longer.

In spite of Lady Meecham's predictions, Lord Eastcott was not in the least disturbed that Miss Lyford's two brothers were to be joining them. He had already determined that the elder was Felicity's legal guardian and he could not but feel that it would be useful to have that gentleman on his side. Surely he could charm Lyford, if he set his mind to it? Lord Eastcott sadly misjudged the case, of course, but then he had never met Richard.

Actually, the evening began rather suspiciously. The party now consisted of Lady Meecham, Felicity, General Sutcliffe, Lord Eastcott, Richard, and Neil and it was arranged that they would all meet at the box Eastcott had reserved at Vauxhall Gardens. General Sutcliffe escorted Lady Meecham, of course, in Harry's carriage, while he and Felicity were let off at the Westminster gate to take sculls across the river to the gardens. Nothing could have delighted Felicity more. For his part, Richard was pleased to see that such an eminently respectable gentleman as the general was to be a part of their party. *That* gentleman, in turn, upon being introduced to Neil, was delighted to have the chance to question a young military fellow fresh from the "*thick* of it," and contrast today's battles with conditions in *his* youth. While with three such handsome gentlemen to defer to her, Lady Meecham could scarcely be displeased.

Cora was, in fact, feeling splendid. From her vantage point at the front of the supper box, Lady Meecham could nod to all her friends and exchange compliments with a favoured few. One young dandy who drew a glare of displeasure from her over the inordinate height of his shirt points was moved to say that one might take the old lady for royalty, so arrogantly did she survey the crowd!

Just as she was beginning to wonder, however, what had happened to delay Felicity and her nephew, Lady Meecham spied them approaching the box. They made, she thought with satisfaction, a very attractive couple. Aloud, however, she said sharply, "Lyford! Your sister."

"Hallo. Is that Lord Eastcott?" Neil asked with interest. "Seems to be getting on very well with her."

A glare from Richard silenced Neil as the pair came within hearing range. Introductions were soon performed and Richard found himself agreeably surprised by Lord Harry. It was otherwise with Neil, and he noted with relief that although Felicity was friendly toward Eastcott, she was not excessively so. Indeed, she was just as likely to bestow a warm smile on any one of her many admirers who came up to the box to greet her as she was to smile at Lord Harry.

In spite of his views concerning Worldly Success,

even Richard could not conceal a certain pride in Felicity's evident popularity. He only unbent sufficiently, however, to observe to Neil that at least Felicity appeared to be comporting herself with becoming modesty. To which the captain snorted, "Doing it much too brown, Richard! When has Fay ever given us cause to worry?"

"There is a certain levity about her that I cannot like," Richard answered stiffly.

"Oh, take a damper!" Neil began, when Lady Meecham's voice cut him short.

"Good God!" she exclaimed.

All five heads turned to see what she was staring at. Felicity was the first to recover. "Lady Eastcott and Mr. Matthews. And Lady Woodhall and Sir Anthony," she said blankly.

"Is this your doing?" Lady Meecham asked Eastcott sharply.

Harry flicked a piece of lint from his sleeve as he said lazily, "My dear aunt, I am not crazy!"

At that moment, the two approaching couples saw each other and came to an abrupt halt a few yards short of Eastcott's box. "Theresa!" Lady Woodhall said in a voice that managed to convey both outrage and failing health.

"Alice," her sister-in-law responded sweetly, "and Anthony. How delightful to see you. May I make my friend, Mr. Matthews, known to you?"

The poor man was obviously acutely embarrassed, but he nevertheless attempted a deep bow. Lady Woodhall merely tilted her chin higher and answered coldly, "No, Theresa, you may not!"

Sir Anthony stepped into the breach. "How do you do, sir?"

Mr. Matthews gratefully shook the hand Sir Anthony extended to him and said, "Well, now, that's very kind of you and I won't say it ain't."

"Theresa!" Lady Woodhall's shrill voice intruded. "I cannot believe my eyes!"

Lady Eastcott looked down at her dress of green crepe. With more than a little complacency she surveyed the long, close sleeves and high ruffled neck. "Why?" she asked provocatively. "What were you expecting, Alice? Damped muslins and painted toenails? It's a trifle chilly for that, don't you think?"

In the moment of outraged silence that followed this question, Richard's voice rang out clearly. "Good God, Felicity! Is this the sort of company you find yourself in, in London?"

As Lyford turned a deep crimson, nine pairs of eyes turned to stare at him. "*Who* are you?" Lady Woodhall asked majestically.

No one, it seemed, was eager to answer this question. General Sutcliffe, however, knew his duty and was not one to shirk it. "Must introduce *everyone*," he said loudly.

With a rather harassed look, General Sutcliffe did so. Lady Woodhall unbent sufficiently to address Richard. "You may well ask," she said sweetly, "what my sister is about, allowing Miss Lyford to consort with a man of Eastcott's reputation. Even his parentage, I believe, has been called into question."

"Only by you, my dear aunt," Harry immediately retorted.

There was another appalled silence and this time Sir Anthony broke it. He looked directly at Richard and said, deliberately, "As Miss Lyford's brother and guardian, you no doubt expect an explanation. Very well, to put the matter bluntly, my mother has always believed that Harry—Lord Eastcott—was the product of an affair between his mother, Lady Eastcott, and my father. May I add that, as Harry said, only my mother has ever suggested such an absurd tale." Sir Anthony paused and looked at Lady Woodhall, who stood rigid with fury. Peremptorily he said, "Come, Mother. You asked me to escort you to Vauxhall, and I have. Let us please find our own box."

They withdrew and Harry turned to the other couple. "Mama, Mr. Matthews, will you join us?"

"Yes," she said.

"No," he said.

The answers came simultaneously. Then Mr. Matthews cleared his throat. "I take it very kindly in you, my boy, to ask us, but we won't be wanting to embarrass you. We only came for a walk through the Gardens anyway."

Impulsively, Felicity said, "Please do join us, sir. We really would like you to. Perhaps you might tell us about some of your travels."

At that, Mr. Matthews brightened. "Well, so I might. Very well, then, if you're sure you want us."

A place was made for them and Felicity, aware that at least three members of the box were furious with her, defiantly chatted with Lady Eastcott.

In spite of a carefully planned menu that included the justly popular Vauxhall ham shavings and rack punch, the meal could not have been said to be a comfortable one. Spaced as the supper boxes were, in two facing semicircles, the Eastcott party was certain to be in view of Sir Anthony's box. It was inevitable, moreover, that Mr. Matthews' genial presence and booming voice should draw the notice of a great many other people as well. As a result, the suggestion that the members of the party take a stroll among the garden paths as their table was cleared met with more enthusiasm than might have been expected. Then, somehow, the group dissolved into three or four smaller ones and Felicity found herself deftly drawn apart by Lord Eastcott.

No one could have called Harry *castaway*, precisely, but it was undeniable that he had indulged a trifle freely in the rack punch. This, combined with a defiance of convention that his aunt, Lady Woodhall, always aroused in him, caused Lord Eastcott to choose one of the most dimly lit paths. Unaware of Eastcott's mood, Felicity made no protest. They paused, a few minutes later, by one of the fountains and Harry said quietly, "You know, Miss Lyford, you are a most unusual young woman." He took her chin in his hand and added, "I've been wanting to do this for a long time."

Then, before Felicity knew what he was about, Eastcott kissed her. She ought, she reflected later, to have slapped him soundly. But it was, in truth, her first kiss and she had been too stunned to do more than say uncertainly, "Lord Eastcott?"

What she might have done next, Felicity never knew, for suddenly a hand grabbed Lord Harry's shoulder and separated them and Felicity found herself facing a furious Sir Anthony. "Is it your custom, Harry, to force yourself on young girls?" he sneered. "It's time, I think, you were taught a lesson!"

Frightened by the anger on Sir Anthony's face, Felicity grabbed his arm as he took a step toward Eastcott. "No!" she said, her one thought to prevent violence. "There was no question of force!"

Startled, Sir Anthony looked down at Felicity. Her pale face was turned up to his and he said, roughly, "Are you so free with your kisses, then?"

And before she knew what he intended, Felicity found herself caught in a rough embrace, Sir Anthony's fierce lips on hers. Appalled, she felt herself responding, an unaccustomed warmth spreading through her. Then it was over—this time Lord Harry having separated the pair. Through a haze of mortified tears, Felicity heard Eastcott say, "I don't advise you to try that again, cousin. Miss Lyford is here under *my* protection." When Sir Anthony did not answer, Eastcott continued roughly, "Look at her! Do you honestly believe Felicity enjoys being mauled about?"

"She did not object when you did so," Woodhall said stiffly.

Harry moved to put an arm around Felicity, who was still crying. "You've mistaken the matter, cousin," Eastcott said silkily. "The cases are not at all the same. Miss Lyford is betrothed to me."

Felicity was startled, but did not deny it. There would be time enough, later, to straighten out the matter. Now she only wanted to escape. Icily, Sir Anthony bowed. "Pray accept my felicitations, Miss Lyford, and my apologies."

Then he was gone and Felicity found a large handkerchief thrust into her hands. "Here, Miss Lyford. Best dry your face before someone comes along," Eastcott said urgently. When she had done so, he said easily, "I'm sorry, but I couldn't think what else to say to Tony."

"It doesn't matter," she said dully. "Let us simply

forget what happened. *All* of it. And now I should like to join the others."

In spite of her efforts, Felicity could not remove all traces of her distress. Had it not been for the presence of General Sutcliffe and Lady Meecham, Felicity would, she knew, have been subjected to rigorous questioning by Richard and no doubt had a peal rung over her. As it was, he contented himself with maintaining a stern silence for the entire ride back to Lady Meecham's townhouse. There he warned Felicity that he would call on her in the morning for a *serious* discussion of her affairs. She was too distraught to care. Sensitive, as always, to his sister's mood, Neil said anxiously, "You will take care, won't you, Fay?"

"Of course," she tried to reassure him.

Neil frowned. "I wish I didn't have to leave at dawn. Oh, well, Richard's here and I don't see that anything terrible could happen while you have him to turn to, do you?"

X

Richard Lyford was deeply concerned. He admired
Felicity very much and, in general, considered her a
most satisfactory sister. Her understanding was excellent, the tone of her mind nice, and her appearance
pleasing. If she was occasionally overly given to levity
it was, he felt, only because of her youth. Marriage
with a suitably serious and mature gentleman would
soon cure that. But that was the rub. *Would* Felicity
find such a husband? She was, he felt, ill prepared to
be cast into the midst of the ton with its hardened
libertines such as Lord Eastcott. And yet this was one
of the two gentlemen Lady Meecham wished Felicity
to marry. Sir Anthony was, Richard considered, somewhat better, but only somewhat. His few hours in
London, moreover, had been sufficient to put Lyford
in possession of the information that bets were being
laid at White's and other gaming halls as to whom his
sister would marry. Currently, the odds favoured
Lord Eastcott not only because he was felt to have
such excellent address, but because the desperation of
his situation must no doubt lend him greater fluency.

All of London appeared to know about her ladyship's will.

It was therefore in an exceedingly grim mood that Richard Lyford presented himself at Lady Meecham's townhouse the next morning, only to be greeted by the staggering intelligence that, "Miss Lyford has gone out, sir."

"Out?" Richard demanded. "Where? When will she be back?"

Tifton lowered his eyes. "As to that, sir, I really couldn't say. She was with friends and dressed for riding, but that's all I can tell you." He hesitated, then smiled slightly, "Lady Meecham is not receiving visitors either, at this moment. But if you would care to try later?"

Abruptly Lyford realized the food for conjecture that he was providing her ladyship's servants and he straightened. "Thank you," he said coolly. "I shall."

Felicity was, in fact, in the park. She had risen that morning in a rebellious mood, determined not to wait at home for Richard to arrive and scold her. Instead, she had dressed for an engagement made several days earlier to ride in the park with Druscilla Marshall. True to her promise at the start of the Season, Serena Marshall had introduced Felicity to her daughter and frequently chaperoned both girls. Druscilla and Felicity got on famously, particularly as Druscilla's fiancé, Major Crispin Palmer, evinced not the slightest interest in Miss Lyford.

Major Palmer was with the two girls that morning, when matters came to a head. The three were riding and discussing Major Palmer's imminent return to the continent, and his likelihood of encountering Neil, when a figure on horseback came galloping toward them. In astonishment, all three reined in. "Lord East-cott!" Felicity gasped, the first to identify the fellow. "But he hates to ride!"

"That," said Major Palmer disapprovingly, "must be evident to anyone who sees him!"

To be sure, Lord Harry's seat was rather precarious, but he reached them without mishap and managed to halt his horse a scant few feet away. "Felicity! Miss Lyford! I must speak with you at once."

Major Palmer, who was actually a year younger than his lordship, said icily, "Really, Eastcott? Next I suppose you shall tell us you wish to speak with Miss Lyford alone! I——"

Eastcott cut him short. "Yes, yes, major, that is precisely what I mean to tell you. And I wish you will hold our horses while I do speak with her."

His eyes gaped in appalled anger as Palmer said, "Impossible! The impropriety of it, Eastcott! I am astonished you could suggest such a thing! "

Harry had recovered some of his poise, however, and he said coolly, "Are you? I should have guessed there was nothing I could do that would surprise you, so long as it was offensive."

Hastily Felicity interrupted. "Please, major, I am sure the matter truly is urgent or Lord Eastcott would not have asked." She looked around, then indicated a clump of trees near the bridle path. "We'll stand over there and you will be able to see us quite clearly," she said.

Before Palmer could object, Druscilla leaned over and grabbed the bridle of Felicity's horse. A twinkle in her eyes, Druscilla said quickly, "The perfect solution!"

Equally quickly, Felicity slid to the ground, needing no one to catch her. The distressed and astonished major found the reins of Eastcott's horse thrust in his hands and he realised the pair of them were indeed headed for the clump of trees as though they couldn't even hear his protests! Felicity felt a strong desire to laugh, particularly as Lord Harry was muttering something about the disagreeability of horses. She suppressed her laughter, however, and said instead, "You wished to speak with me, Lord Eastcott?"

"Do you think I would have gotten up on a horse and let it gallop with me if I didn't?" he asked ironically. He paused as though not quite certain how to tell Felicity what he had to say. Finally he chose honesty. "I believe you know about my aunt's will, Miss Lyford?" She nodded and he went on, "Then you know that it would be to my advantage to marry before Woodhall. Well, I have just seen Tony and he has proposed to Miss Carrington and been accepted, so matters are now urgent. Miss Lyford, will you marry me?"

Felicity felt her head spinning. Sir Anthony . . . betrothed? Somehow she managed a harsh laugh. "A most flattering offer, Lord Eastcott!"

He flushed. "Dammel Beg pardon, Miss Lyford, but that wasn't how I meant it. Under any circumstances I should be honoured to marry you and, had it not been for this, I should have gone far more slowly." Harry paused, aware that he was still making a muddle of the matter. He took a deep breath and began again. "Miss Lyford, I could have come to you and told you that I loved you *à corps perdu* and asked you to marry me and I think you would have said yes. But you would also have heard, before the day was out, that my cousin had betrothed himself to Miss Carrington. You are not stupid, Miss Lyford, you would have guessed my motives. How would you have felt? I do you the honour of being honest with you. If our affections are not yet deeply attached, they may still become so. Even if they did not, I believe we should rub along tolerably well together. Miss Lyford—Felicity—will you marry me?"

Felicity answered slowly but firmly, "No, Lord Eastcott, I cannot."

"What?" His voice was incredulous. "Why not?"

Felicity stared at the buttons on his coat as she said, in a small voice, "I don't know why not. I only know I can't."

Eastcott stared at her, frowning. "Is it because of my aunt's will?" he suggested. Felicity shook her head and Harry asked, "Is there someone else? Need more time to consider?"

"No."

With a voice that seemed more puzzled than angry, Harry said, "You've been eager enough to dance with me, talk with me, attend the theatre with me. Last night you even let me kiss you. So why won't you marry me?"

Felicity blushed. "Pray, don't speak of last night!"

She could not, she found, meet Lord Eastcott's eyes. Nor could she answer his questions. Certainly the match would be, in worldly terms, an excellent one for her. How could Felicity explain that this attentive, so very handsome man made her uneasy?

Had Lord Eastcott been some twenty years older, Felicity might have seen at once that he was like

Lord Sterne and understood the reasons for her uneasiness. As it was, however, she did not, and only knew that she must refuse him. Eastcott, who was watching her face closely, drew his own conclusions and said heavily, "There *is* someone else, isn't there? Someone you would marry if he asked you?"

Felicity was about to deny it when Sir Anthony's face came into her mind and suddenly she knew that had he been the one to ask her, she would not have hesitated. Sick with realisation that she was in love with a man who considered her a child, more a nuisance than anything else, Felicity forgot Lord Harry's presence. How could it have happened? How could she have fallen in love with a man who was now betrothed to someone else? Felicity recalled the times he had danced with her and teasingly called her "little one." She also recalled, with a wry smile, the far more frequent occasions when they had been at dagger-points and he had called her "impossible" and "a wretched hoyden." How absurd that her heart should betray her and fall in love with this impossible man! Well, thought Felicity grimly, at the very least she must never allow Sir Anthony to suspect how she felt.

Eastcott, however, more than suspected. Meticulously polite, his voice devoid of emotion, Harry said, "Shall I restore you to your companions, Miss Lyford?"

With a start, Felicity came out of her reverie and looked up at his lordship. He was smiling wryly and she said frankly, "I must say, you're taking this very well!"

"Am I?" he said gently. "I should have said I was a realist."

Felicity hesitated. Then, earnestly, she said, "I *am* honoured that you asked me, Lord Eastcott. Even if it was for the sake of your aunt's will. There must be so many young ladies who would be happy to marry you!"

Harry merely bowed. In fact, however, he was well aware that while there were a few ladies who would be willing to marry him, not one had a mother who would allow it. It was, moreover, rather late to begin courting some other chit. Especially as all of London was aware how particular he had been in his attentions to Miss Lyford. Nevertheless, Lord Harry gracefully escorted Felicity back to Driscilla and the major. He even contrived, in that short time, to make her laugh. Under Palmer's disapproving gaze, Harry helped Felicity mount. Then, as briefly as possible, he took his leave. Matters were urgent.

As soon as Eastcott was gone, Major Palmer turned to address Felicity. In his sternest voice he said, "Must tell you, Miss Lyford, Lord Eastcott ain't quite the thing. Know he's her ladyship's nephew and you've got to be polite to him, but must be careful. As it is, the tattle-boxes have taken the notion he's dangling after you; don't want to give them any more to gossip about! It simply won't do, Miss Lyford."

Felicity stared at the back of her hands as she said, "I doubt that his lordship will be so particular in his attentions in the future."

Affronted, Major Palmer cut short their ride. Felicity should, perhaps, have explained, but it seemed to her perilously like boasting to disclose offers one has declined. Instead, she once more began asking the major about his journey.

As Tifton opened the door to Felicity a short time

later, he looked most distressed. "Her ladyship is asking for you," he said without preamble. "In the drawing room."

"Thank you, Tifton."

"Quite welcome, miss. Oh, and miss? If I may be so bold," he added with a cough, "don't take it too serious if she should be in one of her tempers."

Puzzled but grateful for the warning, Felicity mounted the stairs. Could Richard have called while she was out? But why should that upset Lady Meecham? As Felicity entered the drawing room, Lady Meecham saw her and thumped her cane angrily. "So, have you heard the news, girl? Anthony's gone and asked that Carrington chit to marry him! *And* she's accepted. Dorothea came and told me!"

As her ladyship paused for breath, Felicity said quietly, "Yes, I know."

"How do you know?"

"Lord Eastcott told me."

Lady Meecham considered the information. "He did, did he? What else did he say? Couldn't have been pleased."

"He wasn't," Felicity answered simply. She hesitated before she added, "Lord Eastcott asked me to marry him. I refused."

Cora looked at the girl incredulously. Furiously she thumped her cane. "You can't mean it! Turn down my nephew? Are you mad?"

"I don't think so," Felicity said quietly.

"Think yourself too good for him?" Lady Meecham asked sarcastically. "Pray tell me, what makes you feel yourself so eligible and desireable a *parti* that you can afford to spurn Eastcott?"

Pale at the fury of her ladyship's attack, Felicity

tried to explain, "You said at the start, Lady Meecham, that I was not to feel obliged to marry either of your nephews. That I need only meet them and hope that a mutual attachment arose. Well, it has not. You must be content with the knowledge that Sir Anthony is to marry."

"Baggage! Is this how you repay my kindness? You know very well that I brought you here so that one of my nephews would marry *you* before Carrington could get t'other one. Don't want that girl in the family and I certainly don't want her getting my money!"

Felicity tried to speak calmly, but her fists clenched and unclenched, hidden by the folds of her skirt. "Even if I married Lord Eastcott, ma'am, Miss Carrington would still enter the family through her marriage to Sir Anthony."

"Ha!" Cora gave a crack of laughter. "That she-wolf would sheer off, fast enough, if she found her precious fiancé wasn't to get my money after all!"

"Then change your will," Felicity suggested coolly. "State that whoever marries must marry someone other than Miss Carrington."

"A pretty scandal *that* would be!" Lady Meecham snorted. Then, irritably, she went on, "Change my will? When I've given my word to Harold and Anthony that I'll stand by it, no matter what? I tell you, girl, I won't serve Anthony such a backhanded turn! Anymore than I would serve Harold such a turn. *I* have a sense of honour, Miss Lyford." Lady Meecham looked both tired and suddenly much older than her years. After a moment, she looked at Felicity sharply and said, "Very well, Miss Lyford. So you won't have my nephew. He'll never marry, now, and I shall be

faced with That Girl on my hands. But I keep my
word. A Season I promised you, and a Season you
shall have. A bargain is a bargain. But I shall never
forgive you for this. Never."

Majestically, Lady Meecham rose to her feet. At
once Felicity sprang forward to help her. This Cora
would not allow. She looked at Felicity with a
haughty, disdainful stare and the girl slowly moved
out of her way. Lady Meecham swept out of the
room and, as soon as she was gone, Felicity sank into
a chair and began to cry.

A short time later, Felicity still sat there, as she
gazed at the cold fireplace and tried to put her emotions into some semblance of order. The effort was
shattered by Tifton's wooden voice announcing, "Sir
Anthony Woodhall."

Instantly, Felicity was on her feet, conscious of a
futile desire to run and hide. Her confusion was not
lost on Sir Anthony, who looked no more pleased than
she did to find her there. His voice rather abrupt, Sir
Anthony said, "I shan't bother you, Miss Lyford. I
only wish to speak with my aunt."

The coldness in Sir Anthony's voice steadied Felicity. She turned to face him fully and, seeing that
Tifton had, most properly, withdrawn, she said quietly, "I shouldn't do that, if I were you."

Woodhall looked at her with astonishment. His
brows drawn together, he said in forbidding accents,
"Indeed? I cannot conceive what affair it is of yours if
I wish to speak with my aunt."

Felicity took a deep breath. "It isn't my affair. I
simply meant to warn you." She paused, uncertain
how to proceed, then plunged on. "I collect you have
come to tell her about your betrothal to Miss Carring-

ton. Well, to put no bark upon the matter, Lady
Meecham has already had the news and she don't like
it above half."

At this point, Sir Anthony interrupted her. "Who
told my aunt? Harry?"

Felicity shook her head. "An old friend, I believe.
But Lord Eastcott told me, also. He . . . he was
distressed."

"That I can well believe," Woodhall said dryly. "So
Aunt Cora is upset. I collect she doesn't like Lucinda?" At Felicity's nod, he laughed a short, bitter
laugh. "If she has such a dislike for my fiancée, then
perhaps she'll change her will and Harry needn't be
in a taking."

"But she won't!" Felicity blurted out. "Said she
means to keep by her word, even if you *do* marry
Miss Carrington. That's why——"

Felicity broke off, clapping a hand over her mouth,
aghast at what she had said. Sir Anthony stared
steadily at her, idly swinging his quizzing glass with
one hand. "Yes, Miss Lyford?" he said quietly. "That
is why *what?*"

She shook her head, very pale. Sir Anthony smiled,
but the smile did not reach his eyes. "Come, Miss Lyford, you'd best tell me. I shan't quit until you do,
you know."

Rather abruptly, Felicity seated herself, feeling that
her legs could no longer support her. "All right, Sir
Anthony," she said, as she avoided his eyes. "I was
about to say that that was why Lord Eastcott and
Lady Meecham are so angry that I have refused to
. . . to marry his lordship."

"You . . . refused . . . Harry?" Sir Anthony said

blankly. "But I thought . . . last night you said. . . ."
He paused, then sat down also. "Why?"

"I don't choose to discuss it," Felicity said softly.

"Nevertheless you will, my girl," Sir Anthony said
grimly. "You owe me that much."

Aware that her colour was heightened, Felicity
said, "Last night, Lord Eastcott only wished to save
me embarrassment, I believe. I . . . I was too distraught
to contradict him."

"I see." There was, it seemed to Felicity, contempt
in those two words. Nor did it help when Sir Anthony
went on coolly, "Most truly the gentleman. And yet,
today, when he asked you to marry him you refused.
Did he bungle the matter so badly, then? I should not
have thought it of him. Harry, in general, has the
most excellent address."

"Stop it!" Felicity cried at him. "I cannot see why
you are so surprised that I refused Lord Eastcott! After all, you have forever been warning me against
him!"

"Ah, but how was I to know you would have the
wisdom to take my advice?" he said with irony. "Particularly when you have encouraged Harry so
outrageously of late."

Felicity ground her teeth as she said, "If we are to
talk about wisdom, or the lack thereof, sir, perhaps
we should discuss *your* betrothal!"

Anger clouded Sir Anthony's mind, for a brief moment, then his sense of humour won. With a quiver at
the corners of his mouth, Woodhall said, "Miss Lyford, you are abominable! My marriage is none of
your concern."

But it is! Felicity wanted to cry out. She did not.

Instead she said lightly, "No more is my marriage—or nonmarriage—*your* affair."

"You are mistaken," he answered grimly. Startled, Felicity looked at Sir Anthony, but he only said, quietly, "I am well aware that my aunt brought you here with the notion of seeing you riveted to either Harry or myself. Under the circumstances, I should be surprised if her anger did not fall on you. Knowing her temper, it is even conceivable that she would turn you out, in a moment of anger. And while it was not my scheme, I should not like to see that happen to you."

Felicity turned away so that Sir Anthony could not see her face as she replied lightly, "You are the one who is mistaken, sir. Your aunt has pledged to give me a Season and, today, she reaffirmed her pledge."

Woodhall did not answer immediately. Instead he studied the defiant line of Felicity's back. Dissatisfied, Sir Anthony took a turn about the room, then came to a halt behind Felicity. He placed a hand on each shoulder and said quietly, "Is that the truth, Fel—Miss Lyford? My aunt will not try to force your hand?"

Not trusting herself to speak, Felicity shook her head. Impossible to tell him what had occurred! Felicity was conscious of a strong urge to turn and bury her face against his chest but, of course, one could not do that either. Before she could speak, a voice from the doorway addressed Felicity and Sir Anthony. "How touching! But I understood you to be betrothed to Miss Carrington, Anthony."

Hastily, Felicity pulled free, trembling slightly. Sir Anthony merely drawled, his voice harsh, "So I am, ma'am. I collect you disapprove?"

Cora Meecham entered the room with her head

tilted to look up at her nephew. "I do," she confirmed. "I've told you before that I find Miss Carrington an ice-hearted chit who hasn't even the sense to hide the fact. Cold comfort you'll find with her!"

"Then we shall find ourselves well-suited, as I have told *you* before," he retorted stiffly.

Lady Meecham's expression softened so that she was no longer a formidable dowager, but only an old woman fond of her nephew. "Oh, Anthony! It's not true! Harold might be called cold-hearted, but not you. I still remember, if you do not, the little boy who came crying to me because he found a dying bird!"

Woodhall answered roughly, "You are quite correct, Aunt Cora, I do *not* remember! And now you will excuse me. I came only to inform you of my betrothal, but Miss Lyford has told me that the news had already reached you. Good day."

"Anthony!"

"Good day, Aunt Cora. Miss Lyford," he said ruthlessly.

Then he was gone. Immediately Lady Meecham rounded on Felicity. "Is that why you refused Harold? Because you've a *tendre* for Anthony? You're a fool if you did! That girl will never let him escape her now that the announcement has been made!"

"I know it," Felicity said quietly.

Lady Meecham looked at her sharply, but there was nothing to be gotten from Felicity's expression. Then, with the experience of many years, Cora said irritably, "I hear Tifton. With *another* caller, I daresay. Wonder who? Someone to gloat over the news, I suppose!"

She was mistaken. The visitor was Richard Lyford. He paused in the doorway as Tifton pronounced his name. For a moment, no one spoke, then Felicity said, rather uncertainly, "Hello, Richard."

Although one would not have called Lyford a perceptive man, he looked from his sister to Lady Meecham and asked, "Has something happened, ma'am?"

Felicity looked at Lady Meecham, who looked at Richard thoughtfully. "You might say so, Lyford! It has been a rather eventful morning. One of my nephews, Sir Anthony, has engaged himself to Miss Lucinda Carrington and the other has proposed marriage to your sister and been refused."

Richard drew his brows together. "Eastcott? I see. Well, I cannot say I am sorry, Lady Meecham, although I know that you must be. I told you at the start that I thought your scheme very foolish."

Her eyes narrowed as Lady Meecham answered softly, "So you did, Lyford! Have I you to thank for Felicity's refusing to marry my nephew Harold?"

"No, you do not," he retorted coolly. "I will be honest, however, and tell you that I am pleased to hear that my sister has shown such excellent sense. She has not allowed worldly considerations to outweigh her principles. However," he added as he looked at Felicity sternly, "Lord Eastcott must be pardoned for having believed that his suit was far from repugnant to you. I could wish that the same good sense that led you to refuse his offer had also directed you last night! A young lady who wishes a gentleman to hold her in respect and high esteem must not give even the *appearance* of any weakness of principles. Nor allow herself to be led into such improper behaviour as walking alone with a gentleman in such circumstances as must surely give rise to speculation. I make all possible allowances for your extreme youth and innocence, Felicity, but I would be failing in my duty if I did not warn you that your conduct last night was past the line. It is precisely such thoughtlessness that leads to gentlemen attempting to take liberties."

Felicity looked at her brother in distress. Unable to keep her voice entirely steady, she said, "Is . . . is that why Lord Eastcott kissed me?"

"*Kissed you?*" Richard and Lady Meecham thundered together.

"So that's what set your back up," Lady Meecham said with a laugh. "Well, I tell you, girl, you refine too much upon the matter. Harry's a warm-blooded rascal, but so are most men. Don't refuse him for a reason such as that!"

"Please!" Richard interrupted, outraged. "Do not be filling my sister's head with nonsense!" Lady Meecham snorted but yielded to Richard. His face very grave, he asked Felicity, "Did his lordship offer you any other insult? No? Well I am glad to hear it, though I should not have been surprised had it been otherwise. Frankly, I am astonished that his lordship had the propriety to try to make amends."

"Amends?" Felicity repeated, puzzled. "Oh! You mean his offer of marriage. But that wasn't because he kissed me—it was because he knew Sir Anthony had just become betrothed to Miss Carrington. Although," Felicity admitted fairly, "he did tell Sir Anthony we were engaged, last night, when Sir Anthony found us kissing and he kissed me, too, and Lord Eastcott stopped *him* and——"

"*Stop!*"

"Fools!" Lady Meecham once more snorted. "Fools,

the lot of you! Just when I had begun to hope that
Anthony had given up the notion of marrying the
Carrington girl, you and Harold have to do your love-
making in public. And cap it with a lie! Well, I wash
my hands of you, my girl. It's *your* fault Anthony will
marry that she-wolf."

Stiffly Felicity retorted, "Sir Anthony is scarcely my
responsibility, Lady Meecham. Or anyone's, for that
matter. He has been of age for a good many years
now, hasn't he? He needn't marry Miss Carrington, if
he don't choose to."

With awful sarcasm, Lady Meecham said, "Oh, no.
He needn't marry her if he don't wish to. The engagement must be known all over town, by now, but so
what? Let him snap his fingers at the girl and walk
away. Is that what you wish, Miss Lyford? Well, Anthony ain't such a loose fish as that!"

Richard could contain himself no longer. "Lady
Meecham is correct, Felicity. One could not wish Sir
Anthony to be so lost to propriety as to withdraw
from the engagement if the news has indeed been
bruited about."

Felicity stared at her brother in disbelief. "I cannot
believe you place propriety above the future happiness of two people!"

"*One* person," Lady Meecham said sourly. "I don't
doubt Lucinda will contrive to be tolerably happy
once she has Sir Anthony's name. *Who* she's married
to don't concern her as much as *what* she has married. And Anthony has the requisite breeding,
property, and prospects to satisfy her!"

As soon as it was possible, Lyford interrupted and
said severely, "Sir Anthony's future is none of our af-

fair, Felicity. Although I cannot conceive how a man could be happy if he knew himself to have behaved with gross impropriety. However, let us leave Sir Anthony's betrothal and consider your own situation. I had no notion matters had gone so far, and this news must alter my opinions. If his lordship has indeed offered marriage, I must counsel you to accept."

"You forget," Felicity answered swiftly, "that I have already refused Eastcott."

Richard sighed heavily. "I forget nothing. I have considered the matter and decided that I shall speak to Lord Eastcott this afternoon. It is a step which cannot be other than repugnant to me, but I do not shirk my duty."

"Speak to him?" Felicity repeated blankly. "You will not? If you do," she warned him grimly, "my answer must still be the same! I will not marry Lord Eastcott."

"You will marry his lordship or return to my parish in Yorkshire with me when I leave London," Richard told her implacably. "As your guardian, I have the means to compel you. Come, Felicity, you must see that I have no choice? Lady Meecham, *you* agree with me, don't you?"

Suddenly her ladyship looked very old. "I? What have I to say to the matter? I promised Felicity a Season and I do not break my word. But you are her guardian, Lyford, and it is for you to say whether or not she stays. I no longer care." Cora paused and closed her eyes. When she opened them again she said, "Forgive me, Miss Lyford, but I find I cannot bear to look at you, just now. I shall ask Tifton to arrange for your meals to be served to you on trays in your room until I am feeling better."

"I shall of course remove my sister to a hotel at once," Richard said gravely.

Lady Meecham rounded on him and thumped her cane loudly. "No! Felicity leaves this house only to leave London or to marry! Do you *wish* to subject me to further malicious gossip? Not," she said with awful politeness, "that I should be surprised at any harm a Lyford would do me."

Richard bowed stiffly. "As you wish, ma'am." To Felicity he said sternly, "Make up your mind to it. Either you marry Eastcott or we leave London day after tomorrow."

"I will not marry Lord Eastcott," Felicity repeated quietly. She looked at Lady Meecham, whose face was very pale, and added, "I won't hold you to your promise, ma'am. I have too much pride to stay when I know you cannot want me here."

"Very well," Cora answered coldly. "I shall see you once more before you leave." She paused, looking very tired. "I am going up to my room, now. I would never have left it if Tifton had not sent up word that Anthony was here. Good-day Lyford."

"I am going, also," he said grimly. "Think well what you are about, Felicity! I shall see you tomorrow."

Once alone, Felicity quickly came to a decision and, a short time later a young and friendly footman left the house carrying a brief note from Felicity to Lord Harold Eastcott. She could only hope that it would reach him before Richard did.

It was, in fact, late evening before Lyford discovered Eastcott's whereabouts. He found him in a small tavern where Lord Harry was clearly engaged in heavy drinking. His eyes glittered recklessly and, at the sight of Felicity's brother, he waved away his two rather rough-looking companions. Richard's lips tightened in disapproval and the bow he gave Eastcott was a very slight one. Harry laughed and said lazily, "Sit down, Lyford. Since I cannot believe you would choose to frequent a place such as this, I must ask myself if you have been looking for me. Ah, you have. I ask myself why. Can it be, I wonder, that Miss Lyford has confided in you that I was a trifle, er, intemperate with her last night? I see that she has! Ah, well, under other circumstances I might cavil at the looseness of her tongue. As it is, however, I assume you know I have already offered her marriage?"

"I do," Richard confirmed. "I also know that she has refused you. We both have reasons for wishing her to change her mind."

"And?" Harry prompted politely.

Richard frowned. "And I had hoped that together we might hit upon some method."

Eastcott shook his head and sneered. "I can conceive of no solution short of carrying off your sister by force."

"Force? Good God, there must be no question of that! It would scarcely answer the purpose!" Richard replied in shock.

Lord Harry frowned and toyed with his drink for a moment. Finally he said, "*What* purpose? I must confess, you see, that I would have wagered you neither liked nor approved of me. Why, then, I ask myself, are you so eager to see your sister married to me?"

"She has disgraced herself," Richard answered

bluntly, "by her behaviour at Vauxhall last night. A private disgrace, to be sure, but what has happened once may happen again and I don't wish a blot upon the Lyford name. There must be no scandal, not the least breath of one!"

Harry looked at Richard incredulously, then laughed. "I begin to see why Miss Lyford accepted my aunt's offer of a Season, in spite of Cora's hare-brained scheme. Well, don't despair, Lyford! A week or two of having you hanging about London prosing at her and Felicity may well change her mind and decide to marry me."

Richard Lyford got to his feet. "I have already told my sister that she must make up her mind at once. I leave for my home in Yorkshire day after tomorrow. Unless Felicity agrees to marry you, she goes with me."

Harry stopped smiling. "Day after tomorrow, you say?" He gave a sharp laugh. "Very well, Lyford, I thank you for your warning. And I believe I can assure you that matters will indeed be settled by the day after tomorrow."

Richard Lyford looked both surprised and gratified. "Thank *you*, my lord. I must confess, I did not expect to find you so, er, understanding." Then, with a rare burst of perception, he confided, "Tell you what I'll do—shan't visit my sister until late in the day tomorrow, when she's had the chance to think matters over. I wouldn't want to set her back up, you know."

Lord Eastcott's shoulders shook slightly, but he managed to answer gravely, "Once more, I thank you, Lyford."

Richard bowed and turned to go. Lord Harry

watched the retreating back with a grim smile and, when Lyford was safely gone, his rough companions rejoined him. They looked at him enquiringly and he answered lightly, "It must be tomorrow."

XI

Annie Wallis brushed and dressed Felicity's hair with the same care as usual, though neither expected that it would matter to anyone save themselves. Tifton was, they knew, under orders to state that the ladies were not at home to callers and only Lord Eastcott and Richard were excepted from this ban. "Well," Annie said as she set down the brush, "that's done. And the trunks are packed, though we don't leave until tomorrow. You've not changed your mind, I suppose?"

This last was asked a trifle wistfully and Felicity smiled, her face pale but determined as she said, "I cannot marry his lordship, Annie. Nor will I stay here."

Annie, who had encountered Lord Eastcott on more than one occasion when she had accompanied her charge for a walk, was obliged to agree that the pair would not suit. And yet she could not feel that the alternative was a happy one. "Are you content to be going north, then?" she asked quietly.

Felicity hesitated. "No," she admitted wryly. "How can I be, knowing I shall be living under Richard's careful eye and having him forever preaching propri-

ety at me? Or telling me I laugh too much? I don't
know if I can bear it. But I *do* know that it would be
worse to marry someone I've no *tendre* for. Mama
loved Papa and even so . . ."

Her voice trailed off, but Annie was in no doubt as
to what she meant. Privately Annie wished she could
tell Lady Meecham and Richard just what she
thought of them, treating a young girl so heartlessly!
It was not her place, however, so she said briskly,
"Ah, well, Miss Felicity, we'll come about! One way
or t'other, the Lord will provide."

Felicity laughed. "I hope so, Annie! And after all,
Richard will be imploring Him, just as heartily as I
do, to rescue me from Richard's parish." She hesitated, then said, "Don't worry, Annie. Go and see
your cousin."

"Well, if you're sure?"

"I am."

So Annie went. To be honest, it was a day she had
looked forward to for some time, ever since she had
discovered that a favourite cousin of hers now lived
in London. And it was true that Annie seldom took a
day off; no need to feel guilty on *that* score. No, the
only thing that marred her cheerful mood, as she set
forth well before noon, was the knowledge that the
next day would take both her and Miss Felicity far
from London. It was perhaps fortunate that she was
not given to premonitions.

Felicity, feeling rather like a caged bird, bent her
thoughts to the future. She was still at it no more
than a half hour later when one of the maids came
to tell her that she had a visitor. To her astonishment,
she found not Richard, whom she expected, but Lord
Eastcott waiting for her in the drawing room. Before

she could speak, he was bowing over her hand and saying, "Forgive me, Miss Lyford. I did, in fact, receive your note."

"Then you know that it is useless to renew your offer?" she said earnestly. "In spite of whatever my brother may have told you?"

Eastcott again bowed and moved away to stand near the fireplace. Scarcely looking at her, he told Felicity, "I fear my proposal, yesterday, has caused you a great deal of trouble and I came to make amends. I do not wish to intrude, you understand, but I know my aunt well enough to guess that she has taken to her bed in anger and that you are intended to be kept cooped up here alone. I'd wager a monkey she has even told Tifton to say you're not at home." At the accuracy of this guesswork, Felicity bit her lower lip and Lord Harry pressed his point. "In short, Miss Lyford, I came to see if you would care to go for a walk with me? I would have suggested a drive, but you know how I feel about horses."

Felicity hesitated. She did, indeed, want very much to escape the house, but she was wary of his intentions. As she watched Eastcott toy with a small figurine from the mantle, however, Felicity realised that there was nothing in the least lover-like in his behaviour. If he did wish to make amends, there could be nothing more shabby than for her to refuse. It was quite kindly, therefore, that Felicity said, "Yes, I should like to go for a walk with you. It will only take me a few minutes to get ready."

Lord Harry bowed and watched with a careful smile as Felicity left the room. As soon as she was gone he began to pace restlessly. Harry was, in fact, nervous and angry, feeling himself forced into a step

he was reluctant to take. There was, however, no alternative. Eastcott had attempted to call on no fewer
than three young ladies yesterday. All three were
generally held to be desperate for a husband of any
sort. And yet, at all three houses he had been denied
entrance and informed that, for him, the young lady
in question would never be at home. That this treatment was due to his own disreputable activities Eastcott did not doubt, but even here he laid the blame
with Miss Lyford. Had she not encouraged his attentions in the preceeding weeks, he would not have
been so confident that she was his for the asking and
he would have taken care to be far more discreet. He
would, moreover, have cultivated the acquaintance of
other young ladies as insurance. Miss Lyford had
much to answer for!

Nevertheless, when Felicity descended the stairs
again, she found Lord Harry in a most gracious
mood. He commented approvingly on the bonnet she
wore and kept up, moreover, a steady stream of
amusing chatter as they left the house and went down
the street. Tifton watched with patent disapproval
long past the time that a respectable fellow ought to
have closed the door. Had he not so far forgotten
himself, he would have missed what occurred next. A
closed carriage drew up to the curb and the door was
flung open. Immediately Eastcott forced Felicity up
the steps and inside. Leaping in, Eastcott pulled the
door shut behind him and the carriage was off before
Tifton could even realize what it was he was seeing.
Hastily, he shut the door and started up the steps to
Lady Meecham's bedchamber. Someone must be informed at once! Miss Winslow, Cora's dresser, was on
guard, however, outside her ladyship's door. "You

can't disturb her now," Miss Winslow told Tifton decisively.

Tifton trembled as he said, "I must! It's Miss Lyford. She's been abducted by her ladyship's nephew, Lord Eastcott!"

"Have you been drinking?" Miss Winslow demanded. "No, I suppose not, but that don't alter the matter. Her ladyship ain't to be disturbed! What on earth do you expect *she* could do?"

In the face of Miss Winslow's stolid contempt, Tifton backed down, but not entirely. "P'rhaps we ought to send for the Bow Street Runners," he protested.

At this suggestion, Miss Winslow fixed her piercing gaze on Tifton. "Supposing Lord Eastcott *did* abduct Miss Lyford—not that I, for one minute, believe it! Do you think, Tifton, that her ladyship would thank you for setting the Runners on her nephew?"

Completely routed, he said, "No, no, I quite see she wouldn't. But, Winslow, what *shall* we do?"

"Do?" she snorted. "Nothing! After all, it ain't as if his lordship intends to give the girl a slip on the shoulder. He'll marry her, all right and tight, I make no doubt!"

With that Tifton was forced to be content. Slowly he withdrew, hoping that someone would come along whom he might tell. As he started down the stairs, Winslow called after him, "If it's Miss Lyford you're still concerned about, I shouldn't go spreading the tale of an abduction. It'll be her reputation, not his lordship's, that'll be blackened, you know!"

At that precise moment, Felicity was trying to make herself as small as possible in the corner of the coach that was jolting her about. Though not yet free of London, the coachman was making as rapid progress as possible over the cobblestones of the streets. Her eyes were wide with fear as Felicity demanded, "Where are you taking me, Lord Eastcott? What do you want?"

Harry had begun to relax now that the abduction was successfully accomplished. From the far corner, where he slouched, Harry said languidly, "Ah, but my dear Miss Lyford, you already know what I want! Your hand in marriage."

"I won't marry you, I won't!" she hissed in reply. "I told you so in my note."

He waved away her objections with a graceful hand. "Ah, yes, your note. I really must thank you, Miss Lyford—Felicity—for that warning that nothing I, or your brother, might say could alter your resolution. Your brother was equally kind in warning me of *his* plans. That, you see, helped me determine *my* plans."

"I won't marry you," Felicity repeated obstinately.

He smiled. "You cannot have considered. You are in my company and will remain so overnight. You *must* marry me and, frankly, I cannot see that it is such a terrible thing, particularly since I have had the opportunity to meet your brother. The idea of you living with that Friday Long-Face is preposterous! Come, Felicity," he said coaxingly, "I promise you shall find me a most amiable husband, and far from exacting."

"You can't mean it!" Felicity whispered distractedly.

"How not?" Eastcott asked lazily. "Who shall stop me? No one knows I have abducted you and even if they begin to suspect, they will never find us. We are not, I assure you, headed for the border and Gretna Green. Nor are we headed for any of my estates."

"Where . . . where are we going then?" Felicity forced herself to ask.

Again Lord Harry waved his hand airily. "To acquire a Special License from someone whom I believe will prove amenable to providing it. My, ah, ardour for you is such that I find myself unable to wait the necessary weeks while the banns are posted."

Her voice was steadier now, as Felicity said, "I am afraid you will be disappointed, then, my lord. You appear to have forgotten that I am still under age and no churchman will grant you a Special License—or marry us!—without my guardian's consent."

A smile crossed Eastcott's face. "This one will. That is why I have chosen our particular destination. And if you are thinking of protesting, let me add that he would, for me, perform the ceremony even if you were screaming!"

Appalled at the new evidence of her helplessness, Felicity was silent. Fortunately, the carriage picked up speed as they had now reached the edge of London and Felicity closed her eyes as though the swaying of the hired carriage threatened to overcome her, No doubt that also was meant to prevent followers from finding them, Felicity thought bitterly, as she compared this coach to his lordship's own very comfortable one. For his part, Eastcott began to congratulate himself on his resolution. His debts were pressing and it looked as if they might finally be covered. After all, no one would refuse to extend his credit once it was known that he was, indisputably, Lady Meecham's heir. Lord, he would give a monkey to be able to see Richard Lyford's face when he discovered what Harry had done!

Tifton, who *was* privileged to see, would no doubt have given a monkey not to be the one to tell Lyford. Richard presented himself at the house in Green Street promptly at two in the afternoon, only to be informed Felicity was not at home.

"Not at home?" Lyford repeated in astonishment. "But where can she have gone? Unless——"

"If you will step inside?" Tifton suggested with an harrassed expression. Once inside he said urgently, "I fear Miss Lyford has been abducted by Lord Eastcott. I had no way to stop him, you understand."

"Good God!" Richard said blankly. Then, recovering himself, he demanded, "What has been done? Why wasn't I sent for, at once?"

Tifton coughed. "Nothing has been done, sir. Her ladyship gave orders that she was not to be disturbed under any circumstances. As to sending for you, sir, I had not been entrusted with your direction here in London."

Richard Lyford looked very grim. "I see. Have you any notion where he may be taking my sister? How much of a start have they had? Was it his lordship's own carriage?"

Tifton answered Lyford's questions as best he could and concluded with, "I'm afraid I don't know where his lordship means to take her, sir. Perhaps to one of his estates?"

"But which one?"

"I'm afraid I couldn't say, sir." He hesitated. "One wouldn't be wanting to spread this about, sir, but her ladyship's other nephew, Sir Anthony might know. There was a time the two were likely to confide one to the other and Sir Anthony might have some notion what's afoot."

Richard Lyford stared at Tifton icily. "I do not intend to draw Sir Anthony into this affair, nor anyone else, if I can help it. I will do what must be done myself. Where is Lord Eastcott's closest estate?"

That question Tifton could answer and did. He was not inclined to place any reliance on Lyford's ability to stop Eastcott, but at least he need no longer feel the affair was his to resolve. Richard, on the other hand, grew steadily more discomfited. It was, as Tifton had perceived, now his affair, and he was not in the least certain that he was taking the right steps to protect his sister. Lyford was, however, a man of action and thirty minutes later he was on horseback headed for Eastcott's hunting box. He was still well within London when he suddenly spied Sir Anthony's curricle. Richard reined in and hailed Woodhall, having taken no more than a moment to come to a decision. Too late, he saw that a young woman was with Sir Anthony.

"Yes, what it is?" Sir Anthony asked with some surprise as he obediently pulled up beside Richard.

Lyford hesitated, then plunged on in a determined manner as he put Sir Anthony in possession of the facts. When he had done so, Richard added, "I mean to stop Eastcott if I can. Do *you* know where he might have gone?"

For a moment, Woodhall was quiet. Then, gravely, he said, "Perhaps. Indeed, I am almost sure of it. My guess is that Harry has not yet had time to obtain a Special License and that will be an urgent necessity for him. And a problem since Miss Lyford is under age, is she not? I believe I know the cleric he will go to, the one man likely to agree to marry them."

With compressed lips Richard replied, "I cannot like to believe that any man of the cloth would so abandon his duty as to allow such a thing. But I see that you are very sure of your notion. Very well, if you will furnish me with this . . . this churchman's direction——"

"I go with you, Lyford," Sir Anthony interrupted ruthlessly. Then, more kindly, he added, "You cannot stop me, you know. Lucinda, I am very sorry, but I shall have to send you home in a hack. There is no time to be lost, you know."

"But I'm going with you!" she retorted sweetly.

"No!" both men said instantly.

Miss Carrington stared at them with narrowed eyes. "Yes. You really have no choice, you know. If you don't take me, the news will be all over London by tomorrow, I promise you." Abruptly she altered her tactics and said coaxingly, "Come, sirs. You must stop Harry, of course, but think of Miss Lyford! She may well need a woman beside her after this ordeal. And *my* presence must, in some small way, lend her countenance."

The two men looked at each other, neither pleased with the situation. Lucinda's words, however, held a measure of truth, they felt, and finally Richard Lyford said, with some reserve, "If you are determined to come, and Sir Anthony allows it, I must be grateful, Miss Carrington. I've no doubt that my sister's nerves will be overset and it cannot but be a comfort to her to have another female to be of support to her."

Sir Anthony greeted these words with a cynical smile but accepted the inevitable gracefully. "Very well. Is there anything you will need, Lucinda? Should we, perhaps, send a message to your mother?"

"No," Miss Carrington answered decisively. "Eastcott already has the advantage of several hours over us and we mustn't lose any more time. In any case, my mother will know I am with you and that there is no need for concern."

Richard was shocked and would have protested except that he felt it was Sir Anthony's place to do so. Sir Anthony, however, merely smiled another cynical smile and addressed himself to his horses. And so they set off: two grim men and a very pleased woman. If Anthony had guessed correctly, they would easily overtake Harry in time to prevent a scandal, Lyford would take his sister away to Yorkshire, and Lucinda would be in a position to demand that Sir Anthony marry her at once. Lucinda could not but feel fortunate that she had chosen to go out driving with Sir Anthony at such an unfashionable hour. This would put paid to his reluctance to set a wedding date!

XII

Had Lord Eastcott hoped for an entertaining companion, he would have been disappointed. Felicity was too occupied with her own thoughts to waste further time in useless protests or speech. It was evident to Felicity that she must rely on herself, *not* the forlorn hope of rescue. Should she pretend to be ill? A brief study of his face was sufficient to convince Felicity that Eastcott was too desperate for such a ploy. Easier, perhaps, to convince him that she had become reconciled to his scheme? Eastcott had, after all, a certain amount of vanity. Hesitantly, Felicity asked, "Why do you wish to marry *me*, Lord Eastcott?"

Startled, Harry looked at her sharply, but Felicity's face appeared devoid of guile. Satisfied, he said languidly, "Why, I believe we should suit, Miss Lyford. You are a sensible young woman, too sensible to be boringly missish. I, on the other hand, am prepared to grant you freedom to do as you wish, so long as you are discreet, of course. Think, Felicity! As my wife you will command respect, a title, and after my aunt's death, a comfortable degree of wealth."

A tempting offer! No doubt Lord Eastcott believed

what he said. The trouble was, would he continue to be so amiable if Lady Meecham were a long time in dying? Or if, contrary to her promises, she changed her will?

Softly Eastcott pressed his point. "Think about it, Felicity. Believe me, I should prefer a willing wife."

"But you'll have me, willing or not?" she asked.

"Yes. Matters are urgent. But you do yourself an injustice if you believe I want you only because of my aunt's estate."

Felicity hesitated and Eastcott held out a gloved hand. After a moment, Felicity forced herself to place her hand in his and to smile tremulously. Eastcott smiled in return, pressed her hand, then released it and leaned back in his corner. Quietly Felicity asked, "How far do we travel, my lord?"

"A few more hours, that's all, I promise you."

Felicity nodded. Seeing that his bride-to-be had become so docile, Eastcott began to talk about the countryside and the customs thereabouts. He was at his most amusing. This went on for some time, Felicity could not have said how long, but it seemed forever. Then, without warning, Eastcott drew a small flask from his pocket. In a soothing voice he said, "We are approaching our destination, Miss Lyford, and it occurs to me that should you once more change your mind, you might try to enlist the aid of the innkeeper's wife. I cannot afford the risk. Therefore, although I regret the necessity, I must ask you to drink this."

Appalled, Felicity shrank back into her corner as she said, "W-What is it?"

His voice was still soothing as he answered, "Nothing to be frightened of. Merely a cordial with a few drops of laudanum to put you to sleep. I shall need to leave you, you see, at the inn, while I go to procure the Special License. And as I have said, I cannot afford the risk that you might tell your tale to the landlord and his wife. They are no doubt respectable people and might, you see, feel honour-bound to help you."

"I won't drink it!" Felicity said quickly.

Eastcott smiled. "Ah, but you will. Either by force or by choice; I cannot afford to do otherwise." Felicity turned her head away and Harry asked solicitously, "Frightened?"

Although her face was very pale, Felicity tilted her chin up defiantly. "It is the motion of the carriage, my lord, that distresses me. I fear we are travelling far too fast."

Eastcott threw back his head and laughed. "By God, you're a game 'un!"

He was about to add more when the coach rounded a corner. The horses were indeed going too fast and the body of the coach rocked perilously for a moment before overturning. Lord Eastcott and Felicity found themselves tumbled together, the flask lost in the upheaval. Lord Eastcott was the first to recover. "Damn fool!" he cursed.

A moment later the door above them was flung open by a large, rough individual who looked very pale. Still cursing, Eastcott scrambled to his feet, a trifle unsteadily. He looked at Felicity. "Are you all right?"

"My . . . my foot!" she gasped. "I think I've hurt it. I can't seem to put any weight on it."

The two men exchanged glances. To Felicity, Eastcott said, "We'll have you out of here at once. Then we'll take a look at your foot."

Felicity winced as they lifted her, but she was soon settled on the grass by the side of the road. "Which foot?" Eastcott asked.

Obediently Felicity extended her right foot carefully. At the first touch of his hand on her boot, however, a small cry escaped Felicity and she looked as though she might faint. Immediately Eastcott drew back his hand. "I daren't unlace the boot," he told her, "until we have you at the inn and a doctor can attend you. But I promise you that will be soon. Can you ride?" She hesitated and he added, "I'll keep a hand on the horse's bridle and we'll go slowly."

As an answer, Felicity turned even paler and gasped, "My head! It's swimming!"

Eastcott suppressed his irritation and said soothingly, "Don't worry, somehow we shall contrive."

Eastcott and the coachman drew apart to confer for several minutes. In the end the coachman was sent to unhitch one of the horses while Eastcott explained to Felicity, "The town can't be very far ahead. I'll ride in and fetch some sort of carriage or curricle and come back to get you. You'll be safe enough with Rogers. He's handy with his pistols and I promise you no one will disturb you."

Felicity nodded faintly. "I understand."

"Good girl!"

With that, Lord Harry turned and strode to the waiting horse, where he clearly nerved himself to ride the beast. An astonishingly short time later, he was out of sight. Rogers came and stood beside Felicity. "I'm sorry, miss," he said, "ruining your elopement like this, but coaching ain't usually my lay."

Felicity wanted to ask what was, but restrained the impulse. So Rogers was not Lord Eastcott's regular coachman? That argued the fellow had been especially chosen for this journey and would be most unlikely to help her. Well, Felicity had no intention of forewarning Rogers. So instead she simply smiled at him, grateful for the reason, whatever it might be, that had led Lord Eastcott to ride for help himself instead of sending Rogers. Rogers continued to fidget and, several minutes later blurted out, "You'll excuse me, I'll be right back."

He then crossed the road and disappeared into the bushes on the other side. As soon as he was out of sight, Felicity was on her feet running toward the trees on *her* side of the road. She had, she reckoned, very little time before his needs had been vented and Rogers returned. And Felicity had no desire either to be caught or to have the fellow see the precise direction she took.

As she ran, Felicity had no very clear notion of where she was going or what she would do next. But that was far less important than the opportunity for escape. So long as she found a safe shelter by nightfall, Felicity would be content. Fortune favoured her. The woods were not particularly deep and she soon came upon a country lane. Felicity crossed that, also, and kept on, across the open field on the far side of it.

Lord Harold Eastcott was not in a happy mood when he returned to the scene of the accident. Although they had been overturned no more than three miles from their destination, it was evident to Lord Harry that the wedding could not take place that day. Nor, perhaps, tomorrow, if Miss Lyford's foot

was severely injured. The gig, moreover, that Eastcott
had managed to hire was a decidedly shabby one and
was drawn by a slug. Hence Harry's foul mood.

He was frowning as he drew up near the overturned coach and his frown deepened as Rogers
slowly approached the gig, hat in hand. Nevertheless
Eastcott tossed him the reins and climbed down.
"How is Miss Lyford?" he asked.

"Dunno, m'lord," was the mumbled reply. As Eastcott stared at him incredulously, Rogers added defensively, "She done loped off."

Harry's eyes widened. "Impossible! Her foot!"

"That's as may be," Rogers said stubbornly, "but
she's up an' disappeared."

"How?"

"Dunno. Went into the bushes to relieve myself an'
when I come back she was gone."

Eastcott wasted no time in uselessly scolding Rogers. It was his own fault, after all, for not considering the possibility that Miss Lyford was clever
enough to be shamming the thing. As indeed she
must have been if she had even gone as far as the
edge of the woods. Bitterly he told Rogers, "Wait
here," and strode across to follow the missing girl.

Two hours later he emerged, muddy and convinced
that the search was a hopeless one. He had passed
two or three small cottages and farmhouses and none
of the inhabitants had seen Miss Lyford. Or, if they
had, they were protecting her. There was an ugly
gleam in Eastcott's eyes and Rogers made no demur
at being told to lead the remaining carriage horses
into town. He far preferred to face the three-mile
walk alone than travel in his lordship's company. An-

grier than ever, Lord Eastcott urged the reluctant cob homeward.

Had he only known it, twice Eastcott had come within three yards of Felicity. She, too, had seen the cottages and been on the point of approaching one to ask for shelter when she heard something that warned her. Already crouched behind the hedge that lined the road, Felicity drew her drab cloak tightly about her. Eastcott passed, oblivious to her presence. The lane here was a long, straight one and he believed that had Felicity been tramping along it, he must certainly have seen her.

It was not until she heard Lord Harry pass by again, headed the other way, that Felicity ventured to move. And even then she hesitated. No doubt Lord Eastcott had stopped at the nearby farmhouse to ask about her. That meant he was not likely to return since they must, of course, have denied seeing her. On the other hand, he must have given some reason for seeking her and if the reason was sufficiently plausible, the farmer, or his wife, might feel obliged to send word to his lordship that they had found her. Ought she to look farther? In the end, it was the approaching darkness with its early chill that decided Felicity. That and her grumbling stomach.

Felicity gathered her courage as well as the folds of her cloak and approached the house. At her knock, an elderly fellow opened the door. Immediately he called over his shoulder, "Martha! Look'ee 'ere! 'is lordship's niece!" He then eyed Felicity somewhat askance and said, "Would 'ee like to come in, miss?"

Prepared for some such tale, Felicity stepped forward just as a small elderly woman bustled up behind the man. "Yes, thank you," Felicity said quietly, "but what did you mean about me being someone's niece?"

Martha elbowed her husband aside and took Felicity's hand, drawing her toward a fire that burned on the hearth. "Don't 'ee worry, child," she said soothingly. "Have a set. Hungry 'ee are, I'll be bound?" Over Felicity's head, she said to her husband, "It's like 'is lordship said—can't remember 'oo she is, poor thing."

"I know very well who I am," Felicity countered steadily. "My name is Felicity Lyford and, so far as I know, I have no uncle living in the neighborhood. As for how I came to be here, that I remember also. I was abducted by a certain gentleman who wished to force me to marry him, and I escaped."

From the glances the elderly couple exchanged, the way Martha mumbled soothing sounds, it was clear to Felicity that Lord Eastcott had anticipated her tale. With a meaningful stare at her spouse, Martha said, "Now, now, don't fret 'ee, child. George, 'ee'd best go feed the hens."

"Feed the 'ens? But I——" he broke off as Martha glared at him. Then, as though he suddenly realized what she was about, George said hastily, "Oh, aye! Feed the 'ens."

Instantly, Felicity was on her feet. "No! You mean to go and tell Lord Eastcott where I am, don't you? If you leave, so shall I."

George hesitated and Martha placed soothing hands on Felicity's shoulders and urged her back onto the settle. "There, there, child. If 'ee want George to stay, he'll stay. Though why 'ee should be so afraid——" she broke off as Felicity began to tremble once more. "All right. George will sit near 'ee while I get 'ee some food." Imperiously, Martha nodded to her husband, who obediently drew up a chair, and she bustled about preparing a plate with bread and cheese and ale beside it. As she gave it to Felicity, she said, "No doubt it be less than 'ee are accustomed to, child, but it be the best we have."

"It looks wonderful!" Felicity retorted frankly.

The couple watched her eat, now and then exchanging the same odd glance as before. Clearly they thought her demented. Silently, Felicity complimented Lord Eastcott on his cleverness. It was a tale that would ensure no one believed anything she said and her own appearance, he must have known, would lend weight to the charge. Why else would a young girl be wandering about the countryside alone, her hair and dress badly dishevelled? And, in the end, who would take the word of a—a child, as Martha called her, over that of a well-dressed, well-heeled gentleman? Somewhat bitterly, Felicity considered the possibilities open to her. She might, of course, run away, immediately she had finished eating, but the prospect of a night spent on the cold, wet ground was a daunting one. Nor was the prospect of tramping along the lane until she came to some cottage Lord Eastcott had not yet reached any better.

Fortunately for Felicity, she had overrated the couple's belief in Eastcott's tale. Hesitantly, George began to ask Felicity about her family. Quietly, she explained her circumstances, not even omitting Lady Meecham's will. When Felicity described her escape, George slapped his knee and guffawed until Martha told him to hush. It could not be denied that Felicity's soft, well-bred manner impressed the pair and when she had finished her story, Martha pronounced her opinion sagely. "'ee don't seem mad to me, don't 'ee agree, George?"

"Aye," he drawled grimly and gave it as his opinion that it would be criminal to hand Felicity over to his lordship. "For I don't 'old wi' forcing a girl into wedlock! Be 'is lordship never so much a gen'lemun."

"But what'll 'ee do?" Martha asked Felicity with a frown. "'ee can't stay here with us. Wouldn't be proper, a young lady as 'ee be."

"Perhaps I could stay for a few days?" Felicity suggested timidly. "I must send a letter to . . . to someone who will come and get me."

"Aye," Martha agreed. "But 'ee'll have to go to town to get pen and paper for we 'aven't any here." She saw the look of fear in Felicity's eyes and added soothingly, "George'll go with 'ee an' I promise 'ee no one will bother 'ee."

Felicity was too frightened to be entirely convinced, but also too weary to argue. So she nodded. Martha sighed with satisfaction and said, "Ah, but now 'ee be wanting a bed, I don't doubt. 'ee can use this one, by the wall. It be our son Willy's, but he don't be here anymore."

Gratefully Felicity thanked them and, a short time later, allowed herself to be tucked in. She was asleep before she had even half composed the letter she intended to write.

XIII

As they followed the route Eastcott and Felicity
had taken earlier, neither Sir Anthony nor Lucinda
nor Richard Lyford could be oblivious to the attention they drew. The knowledge acted differently on
each of the three. Sir Anthony found himself wishing
that he had yielded to common sense and forcibly returned Lucinda Carrington to her home. She, on the
other hand, was delighted. With no effort on her part,
she could be certain Sir Anthony would consider her
reputation ruined. Fortunately for her, Lucinda had
enough sense to keep the triumph she felt from
showing on her face.

Richard Lyford, who rode beside the curricle, also
deprecated the foolishness that had persuaded Sir Anthony to allow his fiancée to accompany them on this
journey. How unfortunate the poor young lady should
be placed in such a questionable position! And yet,
and yet, his sister, Felicity, must come first; her pre-
dicament must outweigh all other consideration. Richard further salved his conscience by the reminder that
Sir Anthony and Miss Carrington were betrothed

and if the wedding day were set forward what, after all, would it signify?

Lyford would have been less sanguine, indeed he would have been appalled, had he realised the extent to which his sister occupied Sir Anthony's thoughts. Woodhall could think of little else. It was *his* fault Harry had taken this desperate step, and therefore his responsibility to rescue Felicity. He found himself, moreover, forming most uncousinly plans for Harry's future when, and if, they should succeed in catching up with the pair.

In spite of his preoccupation, Sir Anthony handled his horses well and kept a steady, rapid pace. Half-way, he changed horses, commenting as he did so that it was fortunate he always carried a full purse. Lyford stiffened and said quietly, "If you will be so good as to keep an account, Woodhall, I shall natural-ly reimburse you for your expenses as soon as I am able to."

"Don't be a gudgeon!" Sir Anthony retorted sharp-ly. "This touches on the honour of my family as much as it does on yours! Now let us be off—I have my doubts about these horses, but they are the best to be had."

It was soon seen that Woodhall's doubts were justi-fied. Lucinda contrived to keep up a cheerful stream of chatter as they drove, but even she was daunted when one of the pair cast a shoe. Of necessity, the curricle made very slow progress until they could once more change horses. Richard Lyford barely re-strained his impatience and only Sir Anthony's refusal to tell him the name of the town they were going to kept Richard from riding on ahead.

It was well after dark when the party came upon

the wreckage of Eastcott's carriage. Since this blocked close upon half the road, it was impossible not to take note of what had happened. Very pale, Lyford would have dismounted and searched the overturned coach. Sir Anthony stopped him, however, and said curtly, "Never mind that! You can see there is no one about. They will most certainly have gone on to the town. It cannot be very far, now."

"But is it——?"

"My cousin's coach?" Sir Anthony cut him off ruthlessly. "We cannot be certain until we find someone who knows. I suggest we waste no further time in doing so!"

Lyford visibly struggled with himself, but finally nodded grimly. "Very well. Let us go on. But if they haven't heard of your cousin, or my sister, in the next place we come to, we'll come back here!"

"You shall, of course, do as you wish," Sir Anthony said with careful politeness. "Miss Carrington and I will stop for the night in Wixbridge, unless we hear word that Eastcott and your sister have gone on ahead."

With that, Richard Lyford was forced to be content.

The Duck and Drake was the only inn of any size in Wixbridge, certainly the only one prepared to cater to Quality. It was, therefore, not particularly surprising that the innkeeper of the Duck and Drake immediately recognised the gentleman Sir Anthony described to him. Aye, the gentleman was a guest at the inn and, aye, he had three rooms he could place at their disposal, as well as one private parlour. Richard Lyford interrupted to ask sternly, "We wish to speak with the gentleman Sir Anthony has just described to you. Will you tell us where he is to be found?"

Eager to be of assistance, the landlord said, "Well as to that, sir, I'm very sorry, but the gentleman has already retired."

"Rouse him," Sir Anthony said curtly.

"Rouse him?" the landlord asked with astonishment.

Deliberately Sir Anthony raised his quizzing glass and stared through it at the innkeeper. In a quiet but ominous voice, he said, "I thought I made myself tolerably clear. Rouse him. The gentleman is my cousin, Lord Eastcott, and I have urgent business with him. Therefore, once more I repeat, rouse him!"

"But that's impossible!" the innkeeper blurted out.

"Impossible? Nonsense!" Lyford said sternly.

Sir Anthony motioned Richard to be silent. He then asked, in the same quiet voice as before, "You do, I trust, have an explanation my good fellow?"

The landlord looked uneasily from one gentleman to the other. "It were the brandy, you see. Coming on top of the burgundy his lordship had with his dinner. Well, between the two, my boy Jack and I had to carry his lordship to his bed not half an hour ago. I doubt me he'll rouse before late morning."

"Alone?" Richard demanded. Then, as he realised the fellow did not understand what he meant, Richard added, "Alone. Did his lordship go to bed alone? I mean, is there anyone staying here with him?"

Once more, Sir Anthony silenced Lyford with a wave of his hand. It was too late, however. The innkeeper's curiousity was aroused. "Aye, the gentleman was alone. Were you expecting another gentleman, or perhaps a lady, to be travelling with him? His lordship did seem in a very odd humour."

With effort, Sir Anthony curbed his own exasperation and managed to say with a tolerable degree of boredom, "My dear sir, you may indulge in whatever flights of fancy you choose, *after* you have seen to our needs." That got the fellow's attention and, after a moment, Sir Anthony went on, easily, "Good. Now this young lady has had her baggage misplaced and would be grateful if she might borrow a few necessities."

Affronted, the landlord said to Sir Anthony, "No baggage for the young lady? Nor abigail, I'll be bound! In fact, it'll surprise me, it will, if you gentlemen have baggage with you." From the expression of dismay on Lyford's face, it was clear to the innkeeper that his suspicions were justified. He drew himself upright and said indignantly, "This is a respectable hostelry and I'll have nothing havey-cavey here! His lordship's cousin indeed? At least *that* gentleman brought a valise."

With some asperity Sir Anthony cut short the tirade. "Oh, do give over!" he retorted. "What do you suspect—an elopement? Nonsense! Two bridegrooms? I told you that our business with Lord Eastcott is urgent. We had no time to bother with baggage and such."

It was evident the landlord was not convinced and Lucinda stepped into the breach. With her cool, well-bred voice she said, "If you must have an explanation, then very well. We have come to *prevent* an elopement. Or, rather, an abduction. Lord Eastcott was seen forcing this gentleman's sister into a travelling coach and we came to stop him. As Sir Anthony's fiancée, we had hoped that my presence might protect the girl's reputation."

"Well, you're out!" the innkeeper snorted with disgust. "His lordship's coach broke down a few miles outside of town and he's quite alone. There's no young ladies here at all!"

At these words, Richard Lyford turned pale. "He's abandoned her," he told Sir Anthony. "What shall we do now?"

"Do?" Sir Anthony raised his eyebrows. "We shall bespeak dinner, eat it, and retire. I can conceive of nothing more we can do before morning. Think man! There's no moon tonight and you know as well as I that we could barely find our way here, this past half hour in the dark. I am as concerned as you are, but I repeat: There is nothing more we can do before morning."

The landlord, who had been following this conversation with interest, warned, "You'll have to pay your shot in advance."

Sir Anthony sighed and answered wearily, "It only wanted that! Very well, here you are. That ought to be more than sufficient."

It was, perhaps, the careless way Sir Anthony handed the innkeeper an amount twice the exorbitant charge he had intended to ask for that changed the fellow's demeanour. It would be too much to say that the landlord became affable, but there was at least a degree of respect in his manner as he escorted them to the private parlour they had requested. He then withdrew to see what food might be fetched up from the kitchen and promised, in addition, that his wife would provide a few things for the young lady. When he was gone, Lucinda said thoughtfully, "Could it all be a hum? Could Miss Lyford simply have run away from Lady Meecham's house?"

Immediately Richard Lyford retorted, "No! Her ladyship's butler was quite clear as to what he saw. Far more likely he abandoned her somewhere!"

"Don't be absurd!" Lucinda answered pettishly. "Recollect that if he abducted your sister at all, it was to marry her. Why, then, would he abandon her?"

Richard nodded. "There is some sense in what you say. Perhaps he has not abandoned Felicity, but locked her away somewhere until he can acquire a Special License."

"What do you think, Anthony?" Lucinda appealed to him prettily.

Woodhall smiled grimly. "I believe Harry abducted Miss Lyford wih the intention, as you say, of marriage. His very presence here, in Wixbridge, argues for that theory. I incline, moreover, to Lyford's notion that Harry has hidden her somewhere nearby rather than risk bringing her to so public a place as an inn."

"But where is she, then?" Richard demanded.

"I don't know," Sir Anthony replied with a frown. "So far as I know, he has neither land nor acquaintances here, with the exception of his uncle, the Bishop of Wixbridge. In any event, it seems useless to speculate. In the morning we will ask my cousin and I assure you, he will answer!" There was no mistaking the threat in Woodhall's voice. He went on, rather more calmly, "It is a simple enough matter to direct the landlord to rouse us the moment Harry shows signs of stirring, *not* that we are likely to oversleep him. I see nothing else we may accomplish before then."

"Just so," Lucinda said approvingly. "I, for one, will

be grateful for my bed. I only hope the sheets will prove to have been well aired."

As promised, Lucinda sought her bed directly after the dinner, which was a tolerable one, and left the two men to the excellent brandy Lord Eastcott had already discovered. Forewarned, however, Lyford and Woodhall were more moderate in their consumption of the potent stuff. "Tell me," Sir Anthony said gently, once Miss Carrington had retired, "why did my cousin take such action? Had you, perhaps, told him you would not consent to marriage between himself and your sister? I cannot otherwise understand such a desperate step."

Affronted, Richard answered stiffly, "On the contrary, Sir Anthony, I informed both of them that if Felicity did not choose to accept his lordship's offer of marriage then I should have no alternative but to take her back to Yorkshire with me. We were to have left tomorrow."

"She would have gone?" Sir Anthony asked with surprise.

"Of course!" Richard retorted. "You forget I am her legal guardian."

"I had not realised she was so obedient," Woodhall murmured dryly.

"Felicity has her pride," Richard said stiffly. "Her ladyship was quite outspoken in her anger that my sister would not marry Eastcott."

Sir Anthony sat upright, gripping his glass of brandy, and said harshly, "Indeed? And yet your sister still refused Harry? Why?"

Richard sighed heavily. "I cannot say. But she no longer has any choice, I fear. Even Miss Carrington's presence cannot sufficiently minimize the irregularity of her position. Fortunately there is, you have said, someone here who can provide the necessary Special License."

"Tell me," Sir Anthony said sarcastically, "if you are so willing to see your sister wed to my cousin, why did you bother to come and try to stop Harry?"

"If we could have overtaken them and returned to London before nightfall, matters would have been quite different. Surely you can see *that*," Richard answered calmly. "You cannot believe I would have wished to see Felicity forced into a union that was distasteful to her. However, matters have gone too far. I would be a very poor guardian if I allowed her to ruin herself, as she would if she returned now, unwed. You know society as well as I do, Sir Anthony. The only hope is that our presence might quiet some of the gossip over the hastiness of this marriage," Richard hesitated, then said, sternly, "I don't wish to seem impertinent, Sir Anthony, but I should also be failing in my duty if I did not point out to you that it might be wise for you to avail yourself of the services of this Bishop of . . . of Wixbridge to obtain a Special License for yourself and Miss Carrington. Her position is also highly irregular, I fear."

Sir Anthony regarded Richard steadily with eyes that seemed almost haunted. So much so that Lyford wondered if Sir Anthony had not imbibed more freely than he, Richard, had realised. Sir Anthony's words seemed to confirm this suspicion. "I . . . don't . . . know . . . what . . . I . . . shall . . . do." Suddenly he smiled a humourless smile and said, "No, Lyford, I'm not castaway. I simply don't know what I shall do about Miss Carrington. I wish I had never brought her here!"

"Then why did you?" Lyford demanded bluntly.
"In fact, Sir Anthony, why are you here at all? Do not
misunderstand, I am very grateful for your aid. I
simply cannot conceive what affair this is of yours.
Granted he is your cousin, however——" Abruptly
Richard broke off, then went on sternly, "I am aware,
Sir Anthony, of the nature of Lady Meecham's will. I
hope it is not determination to prevent your cousin
from fulfilling the terms of the will *first* that has
caused you to interfere. I should not like to think it of
you."

Sir Anthony laughed harshly. "Don't be a fool, Lyford. If it were anyone but Fel—Miss Lyford involved
I might well have let matters take their course."
Woodhall hesitated, then said awkwardly, "Miss Lyford was a . . . a guest in my aunt's house and I feel
a . . . a certain responsibility. Although, in any event,
I should be sorry to see a young girl married to a man
like my cousin."

Richard Lyford studied Sir Anthony's face carefully. He was not, in general, a perceptive man, but
neither was he a fool. Abruptly, Richard felt a sense
of disgust. So Lady Meecham had been correct and
Sir Anthony felt a *tendre* for Felicity. And no doubt
she was also correct in suggesting that Felicity had a
tendre for him. But instead of looking forward to
marriage between the pair, Richard must deal with an
abduction by Lord Eastcott and a wedding between
Woodhall and Miss Carrington. Why the devil must
people be such fools? he wondered savagely. Aloud,
Lyford said quietly, "If, in spite of everything, my sister refuses to wed his lordship and I must take her
home with me, I shall endeavour to see that she is not
unhappy."

Sir Anthony could only nod to acknowledge the promise. Lyford meant what he said, but he was a sober, respectable young man and Felicity—Felicity was like a little songbird. She needed to be surrounded by pretty things and to be able to laugh often. Oh, he could picture her in Yorkshire, all right! In a few years Felicity would be a sober, dignified woman surrounded by sober, dignified nieces and nephews. And if someone paused to exchange a jest with her, she would smile politely, but her mind would be on all the errands she needed to run. The vision was appalling but less appalling than the one in which she was married to Harry.

It could not be said that either Lyford or Sir Anthony found sleep easy to come by, that night.

XIV

Sir Anthony Woodhall was, by nature, an early riser. This was not, however, a trait he generally chose to advertise to his acquaintances. They would have been appalled by such extraordinary behaviour. Indeed, as a concession to his valet's sensibilities, Sir Anthony rarely dressed before noon when he was in town. Here, however, he need cater to no one's opinion save his own. It was thus well before nine in the morning when he strolled into the coffee room already neatly dressed. The landlady had taken care to launder Sir Anthony's shirt and cravat overnight, and dry it with her flatiron so that he might have been travelling with any amount of baggage for all one could guess from Sir Anthony's appearance. The waiter, somewhat startled, asked if Sir Anthony were wishful for his breakfast. Woodhall considered the matter, then announced that he would dine later but would have some bread and a tankard of ale to tide him over until his companions should appear. "Very good, sir," the waiter replied, and hurried away to attend to this modest request.

A few minutes later, Sir Anthony strolled outside

and across the road to sit on a bench under a large oak that stood in the centre of the town commons. The sky was clear and the day looked to be warm and pleasant and Sir Anthony found himself wishing he were in Wixbridge merely to enjoy a few days of leisure. That he would find such a program sadly flat was irrelevant. At that precise moment it seemed an appealing notion.

Sir Anthony looked about him with interest. The hour might be accounted shockingly early by the ton, but the industrious citizens of Wixbridge were up and about and had been for some time. Several of these nodded politely as they passed by Sir Anthony, no doubt assuming he had come to visit the cathedral. And indeed his eyes *were* drawn to the imposing steeple at the far end of town. Its dark, forbidding stone seemed sharply out of place in such a small, quiet village and unsuspecting visitors to Wixbridge were sometimes inclined to believe that they were victims of a strange hallucination. They were not, of course. Whatever else Wixbridge might be noted for, it was the home of Sir Bardrick Covell, whose grandfather had been one of the richest men in England in his day. That the wealth had been acquired by spectacular—and irregular—means was one of the local legends. Upon retirement, Bardrick's grandfather, Sir Gilmer Covell, had sold his ships and settled down in Wixbridge. A cautious man, in his later years Sir Gilmer decided to make some gesture to atone for various deeds he had performed while acquiring his title and wealth. The result was the cathedral. Construction was begun during Sir Gilmer's lifetime and its completion assured through his will, which specified that his heirs could receive his wealth only upon completion of the magnificent structure. In the meantime, they were dependent upon an extremely modest allowance. Three consecutive challenges to the will had been defeated and the result was that the cathedral of Wixbridge was built in record time. Sir Gilmer, moreover, had arranged matters so that Wixbridge was granted its own bishop, this churchman to be paid out of Sir Gilmer's estate. There was no question but that Sir Gilmer had died well pleased with himself. Unfortunately, very few bishops were inclined to accept a position in such an isolated village. Those few who were, tended to be churchmen with somewhat irregular pasts. Lord Eastcott's uncle, the current Bishop of Wixbridge, was precisely such a fellow. When it had been presented to him by his superiors that the alternative was an open scandal, Julian Leverton had graciously consented to preside in Wixbridge. Once there, however, Leverton had discovered the townfolk inclined to view him with suspicion and unlikely to tolerate the pastimes Julian had been wont to indulge in. Leverton cursed his superiors but, aware that there could be no other position open to him, settled in, determined to make the best of it.

As Sir Anthony considered Eastcott's uncle, he had no doubt that the fellow would speedily grant Harold's request for a Special License. No consideration of Felicity's reluctance would dissuade him. He was, in fact, more likely to pinch the prospective bride himself and offer to perform the ceremony then and there. A certain grimness drew the lines of Sir Anthony's mouth taut as he contemplated the image of Felicity being married to Harry by an unctuous bishop who only laughed at her fright. If Harry had hurt her . . .

The thought was never completed for, at that moment, Sir Anthony's attention was drawn to the doorway of the inn. Harry stood there pointing to his boots and calling for the landlord. Woodhall was unable to hear the reply, but he saw Eastcott nod and plunge across the road, scarcely looking where he was going. Grimly, Sir Anthony got to his feet and planted himself directly in Eastcott's path. "Hallo, Harry," he said, with deceptive calm.

"Tony! What the devil are you doing here?" Eastcott demanded in astonishment. "No, on second thought, don't tell me. I've the devil's own head and I don't wish to hear it."

"I would have thought," Woodhall said deliberately, "that you would know exactly why I've come."

"Well, I don't," Harry answered peevishly. "What's more, I don't choose to play guessing games at this ungodly hour of the morning! If I discover the fool who banged on my door or the one who slaughtered a pig under my window this morning——" Eastcott broke off, his eyes widening in dismay, "I say. You wouldn't be here to procure a Special License, would you?"

"No, I would not!" Woodhall retorted shortly. "I came to prevent you from obtaining one."

Eastcott froze and his next words seemed almost wrenched out of him. "How, in God's name, do you know about that?"

Slowly, Sir Anthony took a pinch of snuff, gently dusted off his fingertips, then said quietly, "You didn't expect that, did you, Harry? You were very foolish, you know, to abduct Miss Lyford in broad daylight in sight of Aunt Cora's staff."

"Tifton!" Eastcott said in accents of strong loathing. "I suppose he's the one who told you?"

"Not precisely," Sir Anthony corrected him grimly. "He informed Lyford who, in turn, informed me."

"Lyford?" the loathing was even more pronounced now. "Don't tell me you've brought that prosy fool with you?"

"In view of the fact that he is Miss Lyford's brother as well as her guardian, I scarcely see that I could have prevented him from coming," Woodhall observed dryly. Then, abruptly dropping his languid air, Sir Anthony said roughly, "Where is she, Harry?"

"Don't know," was the prompt reply.

"Do you take me for a flat?" Sir Anthony demanded grimly. "You've admitted abducting Miss Lyford and you're here in Wixbridge. You've also as good as admitted that you came to obtain a Special License to marry her. And now to try and tell me you haven't hidden her away somewhere is the outside of enough!"

"Well, I haven't!" Eastcott retorted huffily. "If you must know, she ran away from me."

"Ran away from you? I've no doubt she tried. But do you mean to say you didn't catch her?" Woodhall demanded.

"Tried to," Harry answered indignantly, "but didn't have any luck. Couldn't even find her."

"I think you'd better tell me all about it," Sir Anthony said grimly.

"My coach overturned and she pretended to have hurt her foot," Eastcott replied succinctly. "I rode for help and when I returned she was gone. Chit must have been bamming me."

There was no mistaking the bitterness in Eastcott's

tone. It was that, more than anything else, that convinced Woodhall. "I see," he said quietly. Then, with unmistakeable menace, he added, "I am going to look for Miss Lyford, Harry, and you had better pray that I find her—unharmed. Otherwise, you will find yourself very sorry, I promise you!"

"Dash it all, wasn't my idea for her to run away!" Eastcott retorted. "Can't see why you have to go and find the girl—she'll only cause a scandal."

Sir Anthony, who had started to turn, stopped. Slowly his eyes met Harry's in a way that made his lordship shiver. Evenly, Sir Anthony said, "If you were not my cousin, Harry, I would call you out for that."

"You may not be able to," Lyford's voice intruded from behind the pair, "but there is nothing to prevent me." Instinctively the two cousins moved apart and Richard addressed Sir Anthony anxiously, "Has he told you where to find Felicity?"

"He doesn't know."

"*Doesn't know?*" Lyford was incredulous. "Good God! Has the scoundrel abandoned her? Lord Eastcott, you *shall* meet me for this."

As Richard advanced upon Harry menacingly, Eastcott said with some alarm, "Tony! Make him understand!"

With visible effort, Lyford gained control of himself and turned to Sir Anthony. "*Can* you explain?" he asked quietly.

Woodhall gave a short, sharp laugh. "It seems your sister managed to slip away from Harry. She escaped."

"Good God!" Richard repeated, blankly. "You mean she is alone somewhere? We must find Felicity! A delicately bred young girl alone—who knows what may have happened."

"Oh, do give over!" Eastcott said impatiently as Richard showed signs of becoming hysterical. "She got away from me, didn't she? I don't doubt she'd do the same to anyone else who tried to take advantage of her. *I* wouldn't call your sister helpless, not by any means!"

Lyford bristled. "Felicity is a young lady. The shock of having to deal with such events——"

"I assure you," Eastcott said acidly, "when I last saw her, Miss Lyford was far from overcome. If anything, her mind was indecently alert!"

As Lyford's face took on a purplish hue, Sir Anthony interjected, "He's right, you know, Lyford. I cannot believe your sister would allow herself to be taken advantage of."

Somehow Richard stuttered, "A sheltered young female such as Felicity might not realise, until too late, the danger she was in."

Eastcott snorted and Sir Anthony said dryly, "Miss Lyford may have been sheltered, but she is not a fool."

With narrowed eyes, Eastcott regarded Richard. "You don't appear to know your own sister very well, Lyford. I can't imagine why you want to take her back to Yorkshire with you. You'll both regret it, you know."

Lyford started to object angrily, then recollected himself. Instead, he said stiffly, "That decision must be between Felicity and myself. If she were unhappy there, she need only say so. I shall make it clear to Felicity that she has the alternative, distasteful as it may be, of accepting your offer, Lord Eastcott."

"Oh, no she don't," Harry said positively. "Even Aunt Cora's fortune ain't worth being married to Miss Lyford! I'd as lief marry a she-cat."

Richard Lyford drew himself erect and said, in a ringing voice, "Do I understand you, sir, that after this . . . this *intolerable* insult to my sister, you refuse to take the one course open to you to offer amends?"

Lord Harry bowed and said, with elaborate politeness, "Precisely. I'm not such a fool as to doom both myself and your sister to what must be unparalleled misery."

"Then I perceive," Lyford said uncompromisingly, "that it is my duty to challenge you to a duel. I hereby do so."

The astonished silence that followed this pronouncement was broken by Sir Anthony's quiet voice. "I do believe he means it, Harry."

"Of course I mean it!" Richard retorted indignantly.

"And I suppose I am to serve as your second?" Sir Anthony asked Lyford, who nodded. "May I ask when and where you propose this duel to take place?"

Eastcott and Lyford spoke simultaneously. "Here and now!" Richard retorted rashly.

"No, dash it!" Harry protested. "You can't act as his second. Who will act for me?"

Woodhall regarded both men for a moment, then answered solemnly, though there was a slight quiver to his voice, "Well, as this appears to be such an irregular affair anyway, no doubt you'll next suggest that I act as second for both of you?"

"You are absurd," Richard answered stiffly.

Sir Anthony retorted ruthlessly, "No, you are the one who is absurd! Do you really mean to force a duel, here and now? *That* is absurd. What, pray inform me, do you mean to use for weapons? Or have you, perhaps, travelled with your duelling pistols? And have you forgotten that you are in orders and that Lord Eastcott, much as I may dislike him, *is* my cousin?"

But Lyford was not to be moved. "I have not forgotten, Sir Anthony. If you choose not to act for me, I shall understand perfectly and undertake to dispense with your services. As for weapons, of course I have not brought any. I do not even own duelling pistols, for as you have so kindly pointed out, I am in orders. Under the circumstances, however, Lord Eastcott's behaviour must outweigh my scruples." Lyford paused to draw a deep breath, then said, "The landlord of the Duck and Drake has informed me that he has in his possession a pair of excellent duelling pistols left by a rather impecunious gentleman in lieu of payment for several nights' lodging."

There was a silence as Eastcott and Woodhall finally realized that Richard Lyford meant precisely what he said. Appalled, the two cousins looked at each other. Eastcott was, they both knew, deadly with pistols. A man of his interests had to be. He was not, however, eager to even so much as wing Lyford. Another man might have decided to delope, firing in the air as an admission of his guilt, but Harry would have considered himself a fool to do so when, for all he knew, Lyford intended to kill. Nevertheless, Eastcott was, however tenuously, a gentleman. And gentlemen do not refuse to give satisfaction when it is demanded of them. "Tony, go fetch the pistols," Harry said quietly.

XV

Felicity woke at dawn. Still half asleep, she stretched, aware only that she ached all over, that the bed beneath her seemed lumpy, and that her room had an unfamiliar smell. A moment later, however, Felicity passed from sleep to full awareness of where she was and what had occurred. For this, Martha's voice was responsible. "Poor child's still asleep. Now don't 'ee wake 'er, George, as 'ee go out!"

Felicity waited until she heard the door close behind George, as he followed Martha's instructions, before she ventured to sit up, careful of her bruises. Martha must have been watching for she immediately bustled over and said, "Morning child, did 'ee sleep well?"

With perfect honesty, Felicity nodded. "Good!" Martha said with satisfaction. "Why don't 'ee dress while I fix 'ee some breakfast?"

Once more, Felicity nodded, unable to trust herself to speak. Martha's simple kindness was almost more than she could bear. As Felicity dressed, she could not help thinking about her position. It had seemed the simplest thing in the world, last night, to write to

Sir Anthony and tell him where she was and ask for
his help. In the chill May morning, however, Felicity
knew she could not do it. Too many times he had
warned her to beware of his cousin, Lord Eastcott. Sir
Anthony was also, Felicity reminded herself fiercely,
engaged to marry Miss Lucinda Carrington, who
would *not* appreciate such a claim on his time and attention. Whatever other trouble she had caused, Felicity was determined not to come between him and
his bride. Well, then, she would have to write
Richard. *He* would come and fetch her and carry her
back to his vicarage. And Felicity would never see
London or Sir Anthony again. Well, perhaps that
would be best. Could it ever do other than hurt to see
Sir Anthony leg-shackled to Miss Carrington?

Impatiently, Felicity paced around the room twice,
then came to an abrupt halt. She could not do it. Any
more than she could stay *here*. Druscilla Marshall had
a cousin who lived in the Fens and required a governess. Felicity did not overrate her qualifications. The
months she had spent in London were sufficient to
make her realise that only under the most extraordinary circumstances would any mother consider hiring
as governess a young lady with no experience and a
reputation as tarnished as Felicity must now consider
hers to be. But the circumstances *were* extraordinary.
Or, at any rate, unusual enough for Felicity to
hope her application would not be dismissed out of
hand. Elizabeth Marshall had three small children, the
youngest of whom was a boy. Due to the difficulty
that attended his birth, this child was generally
described to have "problems." As a result, perhaps, of
the boy's tantrums, as well as the isolated location of
Twisted Oak, the family's estate, Mrs. Marshall had

experienced a great deal of trouble in finding and keeping governesses for her two daughters. So much Druscilla had confided just a few days before. At the time, Felicity had paid little attention and, even now, only a blunt appraisal of her circumstances enabled her to contemplate the notion of applying for a position which could not be other than daunting. But if she were to be buried in the countryside helping to care for someone else's children, then Felicity preferred to be paid, and therefore valued, for her work. One hand crept up to touch the pearls in her earrings. Here was the means to pay her journey to the Fens, if Mrs. Marshall should accept her.

Her decision made, Felicity was able to sit down to the food Martha had prepared with tolerable composure. Good manners prompted her to ask Martha about her own children, a topic the woman was delighted to pursue. "There be but two left now," Martha explained. "There be Willy, my son, and Meg, my daughter. 'ee'll not see Willy, though. He be at sea, somewheres, they say. The king's men come and took my Willy up wi' them these two years gone or more. But my Meg still be nearby, just wedded to young Jem this past fall. A fine young man he be, wi' duna-many acres of good farmland. 'ee'll be seeing my Meg afore the day be much older for I've sent George to fetch the girl," Martha prophesied complacently. "It be a good 'ead my Meg has and mayhap she'll know what we're to be doing wi' 'ee. For I'll not deny it's been worritting me!"

"And me," Felicity answered gently. "But I think I know what I must do, now."

"Oh, aye," Martha confirmed, "'ee must write to

the some'un 'ee said would 'elp 'ee. But 'ee must go into town to do that and what if 'is lordship be there?"

"I . . . I've thought of that," Felicity replied hesitantly, "and I thought that if . . . if perhaps your daughter had some clothes I could wear. . . ." She stopped, took a deep breath, and tried again to explain. "Lord Eastcott will be looking for a young lady of fashion. If I were dressed in . . . in country clothes he might not even notice me. At least, not unless he saw me up close, and that I trust I could avoid."

"Aye, mayhap that would do it," Martha agreed grudgingly.

"Then do you think Meg could lend me something to wear?" Felicity asked eagerly.

Martha shook her head. "Best I lend 'ee so'thing of my own." As Felicity looked doubtfully at Martha's ample figure, the woman laughed and said, "Bless 'ee, I 'aven't always looked so stout! More like 'ee than Meg, I was. I'll fetch 'ee my brideclothes."

So saying, Martha bustled off and soon returned with a simple country dress. Martha had not exaggerated when she said that she had once looked very different! With a tuck here and there, the dress fit Felicity admirably. "Ah, 'ee be very nice in it," Martha said with pride.

Felicity looked down at herself and almost laughed at the thought of what Lady Meecham, Lord Eastcott, Sir Anthony, and, above all Richard would say if they were to see her dressed as she was now. Aloud, however, she only said, "Good. Now my hair. One long plait down the back, I think."

Martha sighed at the thought of concealing Felicity's curls but set herself to the task, nonetheless. She had scarcely finished when George came in with their daughter, Meg. Both looked at Felicity in frank astonishment and she hastily tried to explain. As she talked, Felicity stared equally frankly at Meg. The girl was about Felicity's own age but built on generous lines, larger than either of her parents, so that Felicity felt almost like a feather beside her. As she finished her explanation, Felicity impulsively held out her hand and said, "How do you do?"

Meg was too awed to take it and dropped a curtsey instead. She could not refrain, however, from asking doubtfully, "Don't 'ee *want* to marry the fine gen'lemun what Jem says came looking for 'ee yesterday?"

Felicity repressed the urge to ask if Lord Eastcott had managed to scour the *entire* county looking for her, or if it only seemed that way. Instead, she said firmly, "No, I don't. He's not really much of a gentleman, you know. Perhaps your father didn't tell you, but I'm here because Lord Eastcott abducted me."

"Don't 'ee worry," George said grimly. "I won't let 'is lordship trouble 'ee again!"

"Fine words!" Martha snorted, but she eyed her spouse kindly nonetheless. "Best 'ee be going along now. They'll 'ave pen and paper at the Duck and Drake, I'll be bound, but best 'ee be careful. 'is lordship'll be putting up there, I doubt me not."

"Thank you. I will take care," Felicity said soberly. "And if you don't mind, I think I'd like to tell the proprietor there that I'm your niece."

"Aye, that'll be best," Martha concurred. "Asking questions, he'll be, that 'ee don't want answered. But don't 'ee speak, mind, or he won't be believing 'ee. Let Meg tell 'im. Now get along wi' 'ee."

Felicity nodded and suddenly thought of her earrings. Carefully, she removed then and gave them to Martha. "Please guard these for me," she said. "Someone might wonder how your niece happened to be wearing them."

"Aye, I will," Martha said gruffly as she shepherded the three to the doorway.

Outside, the cart was ready and George helped Felicity up onto the seat beside him. Meg was to ride in the back. "If it was just us," Meg confided to Felicity, "we'd 'ave walked. But it wouldn't be fitting for 'ee to. Not in those shoes."

Ruefully, Felicity had to agree. They were in poor shape after yesterday's escape and, even had either Meg or her mother owned a spare pair of shoes, they would most likely not have fit Felicity. Her spirits, however, refused to be entirely depressed; it was too fine a day for that! She was intrigued by everything and, at the sight of the cathedral spire, which was the first thing one saw of Wixbridge, Felicity said, "I collect the town is very large."

"Lord love 'ee, no!" George said with a laugh, but added with pride, "It be a small place, but we do 'ave our own bishop."

"A bishop?" Felicity breathed softly. Then, more loudly, she said, "I must see the bishop. Surely he would help me. At the very least he may be able to advise me."

"No!" George and Meg said together, then broke off in confusion.

"Why ever not?" Felicity asked in astonishment. "Don't you think he would believe my story?"

"Don't 'ee see 'im!" was all that George would say.

After a moment, Meg drew her breath and said, "We don't be proud of it, but best 'ee know. The fine bishop, he 'as an eye for unwed girls."

"More'n an eye!" George snorted. "And not a few wives. Oh, there be tales, aye, and more'n one church bastard hereabouts."

"Hush!" Meg told her father. "That be gossip!" George only snorted again and Meg said cautiously to Felicity, "It don't be our place to tell 'ee what 'ee ought to do, but 'ee would better avoid our bishop."

Appalled, Felicity nodded. If the bishop were indeed guilty of such conduct. . . . She paused and swallowed. In spite of her birth, the bishop might feel *her* fair game if he knew her story, and Felicity had no heart to fend off another assault. Nor was there any certainty that the bishop would protect her from Lord Eastcott, even if the local gossip were mistaken. Felicity could not forget that Eastcott had said this town was their destination and he must have had some reason to believe that the bishop here would grant his request for a Special License and marry them. No, Felicity must consider herself dependent on no one's resources save her own. It was a grim proposal for someone as ill-prepared as herself for independence. Nevertheless, it was better to face reality and act, than sit back and wait for someone else to determine her future. Abruptly, she became aware that Meg and George were arguing.

"Now don't 'ee be telling anyone about the lady," Meg admonished her father.

"And why not?" he demanded belligerently. "Don't 'ee like 'er?"

Meg sighed, "Aye, and what if 'is fine lordship hears of it and be coming 'round to take 'er back?"

George clenched his free fist and said ominously, "No, he won't! I won't let 'im take 'er."

It was Meg's turn to snort. "Oh, aye! Knock the gen'lemun down an' see 'ow fast 'ee find the way to the gaol. And who'll stop 'im from taking 'er away then?"

George merely glowered and muttered, "I never said I would speak of 'er."

Satisfied, Meg fell silent. Soon enough George halted the cart on the outskirts of Wixbridge and helped Felicity down from her perch. Now that she was so close to the risk of encountering Lord Eastcott, Felicity felt herself start to tremble. Meg seemed to guess Felicity's fears for she said encouragingly, "No one would ever know 'ee for a lady, never fear. 'is lordship wouldn't even look at 'ee, dressed as 'ee are!"

Felicity nodded, took a deep breath, and tried to smile. The two young women linked arms and began the walk to the Duck and Drake at the centre of Wixbridge. Meg gossiped good-naturedly as they walked, but Felicity only listened with half an ear. She was too concerned with keeping a watch for Lord Eastcott to care who had how many children. There was, Felicity tried to tell herself, really very little danger that Lord Eastcott would be up and about at this hour. She had almost convinced herself when she and Meg reached the common and Felicity froze, unable to believe the sight that met her eyes. Richard, Lord Eastcott, and even Sir Anthony stood under an enormous oak. Barely had Felicity's mind registered these facts before she saw Lord Eastcott calmly raise a pistol and point it directly at Sir Anthony's chest.

There was no time to think. "Get help, Meg!" Felicity said urgently. Then, with a cry, she gathered up her skirts, raced across the grass, and flung herself on Eastcott's arm, knocking the pistol out of his hand.

XVI

As Sir Anthony reluctantly walked back to the inn to fetch the duelling pistols, Lord Eastcott and Richard Lyford were left to stare uneasily at one another. They were both determined, however, on this course of action, a fact of which Sir Anthony was well aware. With a silent curse on their heads, Woodhall entered the Duck and Drake and asked for the innkeeper. "Aye?" the fellow grunted reluctantly.

"I have need," Sir Anthony said coolly, "of your duelling pistols. I understand you have such a set?"

"I do," the innkeeper admitted. "But I'll not be lending them out to *you*! If there's a duel afoot, I want no part of it. Killing and such like! A fine thing it would be if I was to allow it."

"There will be no killing," Sir Anthony replied.

"Oh, aye. Promised that, have they?" the innkeeper said sarcastically. "And like as not they'll forget such promises in the end. That one or t'other will prove to be an uncommonly poor shot and it'll be too late for promises. I know all about hot-headed young gentlemen and I'll have nothing to do with such nonsense."

"There will be no killing," Sir Anthony repeated.

"Nor do I intend to rely on promises." He paused and a smile crossed his lips. "Perhaps I ought to explain that *I* am to act as second to both, er, principals in this affair."

"*Both of 'em?*" the innkeeper gaped. "You're all mad! The lot of you!"

"Oh, I think not," Sir Anthony answered calmly. "At least I'm not. My companions, on the other hand, are intent upon folly. I wish to thrust a spoke in their wheels with your help."

"Aye, but can you do it?" he asked doubtfully.

Again Sir Anthony smiled. "Oh, yes, I think so. As second for both, it's my duty to inspect the pistols, you see. And I thought that if I removed the ball and left the powder, that might do the trick."

The innkeeper stared a moment, then laughed loudly. "Oh, aye, that'll do it! A fine duel they'll have themselves and neither one hurt! Very well, you may have the use of my pistols. But I'll be wanting them back, afterward, mind you!"

A few minutes later, Sir Anthony emerged from the Duck and Drake, a large, finely tooled pistol case in his hands. As he approached the oak tree, Sir Anthony noticed that both Harry and Lyford appeared to suddenly find their neckcloths a trifle tight. Woodhall came to a halt a few feet from the pair. "You are still determined on fighting?" he asked gravely.

Both men nodded and Sir Anthony opened the case. There was silence again as both men stared at the pistols. Then Sir Anthony said quietly, "I believe you have the choice, Harry. You may rest assured that I have inspected both of them."

Eastcott hesitated, as though nerving himself, then quickly reached out and took a pistol. Rather pale, he seemed not quite to know what to do with it. "Does it feel properly weighted?" Sir Anthony prompted gently.

Harry looked at his cousin sharply, but Sir Anthony's face betrayed nothing more than calm concern. His lordship took a deep breath, then slowly raised the pistol in front of him. It happened to point at Sir Anthony's chest. Suddenly, a small figure threw itself against Eastcott's arm, knocking the pistol to the ground.

"Felicity!"

"Miss Lyford?"

"I told you she wasn't the helpless sort," Eastcott said coolly. Then, "I do wish you wouldn't do that, Miss Lyford."

Very pale, Felicity released Lord Eastcott's arm. As she did so, Sir Anthony drawled, "That was a remarkably stupid thing to do, Miss Lyford."

Felicity turned on Sir Anthony and demanded indignantly, "What was I supposed to do? Let him shoot you?"

With a curious smile, Sir Anthony replied, "There was very little danger of that, I promise you."

Too intent on each other, neither Felicity nor Sir Anthony saw Lord Eastcott bend down and retrieve the pistol. They could not, however, fail to notice when he once more levelled it at his cousin and said, "Come to think of it, that might not be such a bad notion, Miss Lyford."

Felicity would have thrown herself at the pistol again if Sir Anthony had not restrained her. "Must you repeat your mistakes, Miss Lyford?" he demanded wearily. Then, to Harry, he said, "What the devil do you think you're doing now?"

"Threatening to shoot you," Harry answered promptly. "Well, look at it from my point of view! I can only think of two methods of insuring that I marry before you do. And I have already told you that not even Aunt Cora's will is sufficient inducement to become tenant-for-life with a wildcat like Miss Lyford."

"You forget, sir, that you are speaking of my sister!" Richard Lyford said in tones of outrage.

Before Eastcott could answer, a female shriek pierced the air, causing several of the participants in the drama to feel a sense of *déjà vu*. Miss Lucinda Carrington, however, did *not* hurl herself against Lord Eastcott's gun arm. That action was left to Lyford, who took advantage of Harry's distraction to seize the pistol. As Eastcott rubbed his now sore arm and glared angrily at both Lyfords, Lucinda demanded of Sir Anthony, "Just what is going on? The innkeeper spoke of a duel. And what is Miss Lyford doing here, dressed like *that*?" Lucinda's eyes raked scathingly over Felicity and her eyes narrowed as she said, "Lord Eastcott hasn't married you, has he?"

"Good God, no!" Eastcott answered bitterly.

"Not yet," Lyford interjected grimly.

"Never!" Felicity flung back.

"I don't think he will," Sir Anthony said calmly. He placed a hand on Eastcott's shoulder and shook it roughly. "There's no need for such desperate measures, Harry! If Aunt Cora's legacy matters so much to you, then I'll engage not to marry until after you do, no matter how long that takes."

Eastcott's jaw fell open. Then, hastily, he said, "That's devilish handsome of you, Tony! Never knew you were such a sporting fellow."

"Have you gone *mad*, Sir Anthony?"

Slowly, calmly, Sir Anthony turned and looked at Lucinda. Deliberately he said, "I don't think so, Miss Carrington."

"Well, I do! That, or you're a fool!" she hissed. Lucinda pulled the heavy ring from her finger and flung it at him as she announced, "Our engagement is finished!"

Sir Anthony picked up the ring and bowed very politely as Lucinda glared at him, her bosom still heaving with wrath. Lord Eastcott looked from one to the other speculatively. After a moment, he drawled, "Do you indeed mean that, Miss Carrington?" At her frigid nod, Harry went on, "Then will you do me the honour, Miss Carrington, of accepting my hand in marriage?"

Lucinda stared at Eastcott through narrowed eyes. Bluntly she demanded, "Here? Now? With a Special License from your uncle?" Harry bowed, then nodded, and Lucinda said, more than a hint of triumph in her voice, "I accept!"

Quite happy, Lord Eastcott led his prospective bride away in the direction of the cathedral. Richard finally found *his* voice and sputtered indignantly, "The lack of decency! The want of propriety! A veritable hoyden! I cannot believe any man would be so lost to sense as to actually *wish* to marry such a creature!"

"You forget my cousin is desperate," pointed out Sir Anthony rather kindly. "Though actually I suspect they will suit very well."

"I have not forgotten, nor will I forget, *your* irregular behaviour in this affair," Richard replied stiffly. "Please remove your hand from my sister's waist!" As

Felicity started, Richard demanded in the sternest tone, "What, Felicity, has happened to your clothing?"

Felicity looked at her brother defiantly, "I left it with the people who sheltered me, last night. They are around here, somewhere. I had to come to town if I wanted to write a letter and I felt safer if I were dressed like this."

"Your ankles are showing!" Richard replied with awful gravity. "However, it is all of a piece. You have thoroughly disgraced yourself and what my parishioners will say I cannot even begin to guess!"

Her chin held high, Felicity answered, "It does not matter what your parishioners think because I am not going north to Yorkshire with you."

"No?" Richard asked roughly. "You have, I suppose, some other proposal for your future?"

"I am going to be a governess!" she retorted defiantly. "Or . . . or a parlour maid! Anything would be preferable to living with you!"

"Felicity—"

Before Lyford could say anything more, Sir Anthony interrupted them and said, "Surely you must see, Lyford, that your sister's nerves are overwrought? Why don't you take the duelling pistols in to the landlord and give me a chance to speak with Felicity?"

"Duelling pistols?" Felicity demanded as she tried to ignore his use of her name.

"Yes, duelling pistols," Sir Anthony repeated kindly. "You will no doubt be flattered to know that your brother and Harry were preparing to fight a duel. To avenge your honour, you know. What you saw—and interrupted—was Harry checking the weight of his pistol."

Felicity had turned rather pale at this talk of duels, but now her colour returned and she snorted. "What nonsense! Why grown men should stand beneath trees and fire pistols at one another is beyond my comprehension! I thought duelling had been outlawed —as well it should be!"

Sir Anthony laughed, but Richard Lyford was not in the least amused. "I regret, Felicity, that you appear to hold your honour so lightly."

Gently Felicity replied, "I do not underrate my honour, Richard. But I cannot wish to be the cause of any man's being killed or injured. Particularly as I *am* unharmed."

"Not in the eyes of Society!" her brother retorted.

Felicity found that she could not answer Richard. Curtly Sir Anthony said, "I think you'd best take those pistols inside, Lyford."

Stiffly Richard bowed and retreated, with full dignity, to the Duck and Drake. Sir Anthony guided Felicity to the bench beneath the oak. "How could you let them?" she demanded.

Sir Anthony smiled but said, soothingly, "I didn't. That is, they *thought* they were to fight a duel, however I had taken the precaution of removing the lead beforehand. None of us stood in the slightest danger," he added kindly.

Unable to look at Sir Anthony directly, Felicity stared at the ground as she said, "I . . . I'm sorry about Lucinda—Miss Carrington!"

"Are you?" was the cool reply.

Silence. Felicity tried again. "Why were you in

Wixbridge, Sir Anthony? Did you and Miss Carrington also mean to obtain a Special License?"

As he looked down at the top of Felicity's head, Sir Anthony permitted himself a smile. His voice, however, was as cool as ever as he said, "No, we did not. As a matter of fact, Miss Lyford, we came—with your brother, of course—to rescue you."

"Oh," was all that Felicity could say, in a very small voice.

Sir Anthony's next words were even more disturbing. "Tell me, Miss Lyford, are you truly determined to be a governess?"

"If the alternative is to go and live with my brother, then, why yes," Felicity said evenly.

"And if the alternative is to marry me?" Sir Anthony asked gently.

Felicity lifted her face to stare at Sir Anthony. "How dare you make game of me?" she demanded.

Felicity had gotten to her feet as she said these words and now so did Sir Anthony. He took her hands in his and said quietly, "But I'm serious, Felicity. I'm asking you to marry me."

Felicity wished, for the first time in her life, that she were the fainting sort of female. Under other circumstances, no words could have been more welcome than a proposal of marriage from Sir Anthony. But not here, not like this! That she loved Sir Anthony, Felicity did not try to deny. But it seemed to her that a one-sided marriage—as this surely would be—could only mean misery. Felicity swayed slightly, then looked around desperately for Meg. Surely, by now she should have come with help? Surely she would help Felicity escape this nightmare?

"What is it?" Sir Anthony demanded, his voice rough with concern.

Before Felicity could answer, help did arrive. "What be this all about, now? Be there pistols? Meg spoke of three gen'lemun!"

As Sir Anthony took in the vision of George standing there with clenched fists, Felicity found herself enveloped in Meg's comforting embrace. Suddenly the events of the past two days seemed too much and Felicity helplessly began to cry. "There are no pistols, now," Sir Anthony said quietly.

"That's as may be," Meg said bluntly. "But we don't be holding wi' you bothering our friend!"

"That be right!" George said belligerently and he stepped between Felicity and his lordship.

Sir Anthony looked over George's shoulder at Felicity and raised his eyebrows. "Well, Miss Lyford," he said finally. "Am I bothering you? Do you wish me to go away?" As Felicity looked at him, wide-eyed and uncertain of what to say, he went on lightly, "You have very loyal friends, I see." Felicity searched his face for a hint of mockery, but there was none. After a moment, he said quietly, "Believe me, Felicity, I have no wish to distress you. But I would like to talk with you about your future. If you cannot bring yourself to marry me, we must see what we can do to scotch the scandal."

"*Another* gen'lemun what be wanting to marry 'ee?" George gaped. "What's wrong wi' this 'un?"

Both Felicity and Sir Anthony barely heard George. A bit tremulously she said, "Perhaps everyone will be so busy talking about your cousin's marriage to Miss Carrington that I shall go unnoticed."

But Sir Anthony was not so easily deterred. He

held out his hand to her and said gently, "Won't you at least talk with me about it?"

Felicity hesitated and George took a step forward, fists still clenched. "If she don't be wanting to talk wi' 'ee, she don't be wanting to talk wi' 'ee."

Meg, who had been watching Felicity and Sir Anthony, now came to her own conclusions and said briskly, "Do put 'ee down the fists, Dah." Then, to Felicity, she added, "I do believe 'ee ought to go wi' 'im."

Sir Anthony's eyes met Meg's, a gleam of amusement in them. "Thank you," he told her softly.

She dimpled and barely suppressed a giggle. Felicity, caught up in her own confused emotions, saw none of this and Sir Anthony's face was suitably grave when she finally looked at him. "Very well," she said, at last.

Sir Anthony spoke, then, to George and his daughter. "I shall take good care of her, I promise you. You will either find us, or a message, at the Duck and Drake later today."

Meg nodded, and George watched them go without a word. It was the calmness with which Felicity allowed Sir Anthony to lead her back to the inn that reassured them the most. For her part, Felicity found that Sir Anthony's hand on hers was strangely comforting, and yet she could not bring herself to meet his eyes.

When they reached the Duck and Drake, Sir Anthony found the doorway blocked by the broad figure of the innkeeper. "The private parlour," Sir Anthony told him curtly.

The landlord hesitated. He was inclined to favour such a freespending, quick-witted member of Quality, but there were standards to maintain. "The taproom'll do for the likes of her," he suggested hopefully.

Sir Anthony was adamant. "I said I wish to use the private parlour."

The landlord held his ground. "Yes, sir, and very welcome to it *you* are. But not for a young *person* such as her."

For a moment, Sir Anthony looked as though he would like to plant the fellow a facer. Prudence won out, however, and instead he produced a large gold piece. "This *person*," he said quietly, "is a young lady."

The innkeeper stared at the coin, swallowed, and stepped aside. It would be too much to say that his expression welcomed Felicity, but at least he made no further objection as he led the way to the parlour. Fortunately, there were few guests to witness Felicity's unorthodox raiment. Even Richard Lyford appeared to have vanished, although it was far more likely that he was merely exercising an unaccustomed discretion.

As the door of the private parlour closed behind them Sir Anthony said politely, "Won't you sit down, Miss Lyford?" He, however, remained standing, his hands on the back of a chair that faced the one Felicity had chosen. "Good. You look a trifle pale. Perhaps some sherry?" he suggested. Felicity shook her head and he went on, "As you wish. Will you tell me your plans."

Quietly Felicity said, "I know of a woman who is looking for a governess. I have reason to believe she might agree to hire me." Sir Anthony looked at her doubtfully and Felicity tilted her chin up as she said,

"The woman has trouble, I believe, in finding and re-taining governesses."

"I see. And you find that scheme preferable to re-turning to London?" he asked grimly.

"I find it preferable to Yorkshire," Felicity retorted bluntly. "As for London, how could I return?"

"Easily. As my wife," Sir Anthony said, his eyes fixed on her face.

Stiffly she answered, "What you suggest is impos-sible."

"Why?" he demanded roughly. "Am I so repugnant to you? Why? Look at me, Felicity!"

She had no choice as his hand forced her chin upward. "No, not so repugnant to me," Felicity an-swered quietly. "But I am not such a fool, Sir An-thony, as to allow you to marry me out of some misguided notion of chivalry. You would find you hated me before a sixmonth was out!"

"I see." Abruptly Sir Anthony released her and stalked over to the parlour window. His back turned to Felicity and his hands thrust deep in his pockets, Sir Anthony said, in conversational tones, "So you be-lieve me to be offering you marriage to save your rep-utation?"

"Why else?" her voice challenged him.

He risked a glance at Felicity over his shoulder. "Oh, perhaps I am protecting *my* reputation. Or per-haps I still hope to gain my aunt's inheritance."

Felicity laughed and said dryly, "I scarcely think so! Lord Eastcott and Miss Carrington will have lost no time in tying the knot. I shouldn't be surprised, in fact, if they've already done so." She paused, then went on evenly, "As for your reputation, Sir Anthony,

I never asked you to rescue me. I did that on my own!"

Sir Anthony chuckled. "So you did. Lord, I'd give a monkey to have seen Harry's face when he found you had given him the slip! He must have been furious!"

As he spoke, Sir Anthony steadily walked toward Felicity until he was so close she was forced to look up at him. Still smiling, he then looked down at her as though he could see how erratically her heart was beating. Once again he possessed himself of her hands. "Why did you try to rescue *me*, Miss Lyford?" he asked softly.

Felicity tried to pull her hands free, but without success. "I . . . he . . . I couldn't let him shoot you!"

"Why not?" Sir Anthony persisted. Felicity could only look up at him helplessly. He drew her to her feet and said, "There is another possibility, you know. I might have asked you to marry me because I found I loved you, Felicity."

Again she tried to free herself as she protested, "Oh, no you couldn't."

"Why not, Miss Lyford?" he persisted.

"B-Because I'm a scruffy provincial chit!" she retorted, flinging his own words back at him. "I've no presence or breeding or sense!"

"Did I say that?" Sir Anthony asked with amusement.

"You did," she confirmed tremulously.

"I see then why you don't wish to marry me," Sir Anthony said, as he laughed softly. "You can't bear to be leg-shackled to someone who is obviously either a madman or a fool!" His voice dropped, then, suddenly serious. "Felicity, my love, won't you marry me? Or are you truly so indifferent to me?" For a moment she didn't answer and he went on anxiously, "Felicity?"

She looked up at him, then, a smile trembling about her lips. "No, not indifferent . . . Anthony," she whispered softly.

Sir Anthony swept Felicity up in a tight embrace. His lips pounced on hers and, in spite of her so very proper upbringing, Miss Felicity Lyford discovered she had no desire to resist.

They were still at it when someone rapped briskly at the door of the private parlour. "Go away!" Sir Anthony commanded roughly.

Instead, the intruder entered the room without ceremony. In frigid accents, the landlord of the Duck and Drake said loudly, "There are certain persons wishing to see you and your *companion,* sir."

"Who?" Sir Anthony asked without interest.

"I, for one!" Richard announced, his outrage clearly exceeding even the landlord's. "How can you have so far forgotten yourself, Felicity? Are you mad?"

"Perhaps I should explain," Sir Anthony said with elaborate politeness, "that Felicity and I are engaged to be married."

The landlord's jaw hung open. Stiffly Richard said, "I think you forget, sir, that my consent is required so long as Felicity is under age."

"Were you thinking of withholding it?" Sir Anthony asked coolly. "I should have thought you would be delighted to have her off your hands." He paused to look down at Felicity. "We could always go to Scotland, you know."

His face almost purple, Richard fairly shouted, "I wash my hands of both of you!"

"We have your consent, then?" Sir Anthony demanded.

"Yes!"

Only Felicity felt the tension in Sir Anthony's shoulders ease. "Thank you," he said quietly. "I realize you're very angry with us, but perhaps it will be some consolation to know that I think that with your help we may brush through this tolerably well. I propose, Lyford, to take Felicity back to London and arrange to have the banns posted. We will be married from my aunt's house, of course. Unless you would prefer to perform the ceremony in Yorkshire?"

"No, no," Richard said hastily. "If her ladyship has no objection to your scheme, I shan't. But what about this journey?"

Sir Anthony looked at his future brother-in-law and smiled. "Why we came to witness my cousin's marriage, of course. He can scarcely object to *that* version of events, you know."

"Object to what, my dear Tony?" Lord Eastcott asked as he strolled into the room with Lucinda. He paused. "By the way, may I present Lady Eastcott?"

Richard and Sir Anthony bowed, Felicity managed a brief nod. Harry then listened politely to Sir Anthony's scheme. He was inclined to approve. "I felicitate you on your fertile imagination, cousin," Eastcott said dryly. "Rest assured that we shall support your story, shall we not, Lucinda?"

Lady Eastcott shrugged. "Why not? *I've* no wish to cause a scandal for Miss Lyford."

"How generous of you!" Sir Anthony murmured.

"Mad, all mad!" Richard muttered as he mopped his brow.

Everyone ignored Lyford. "It occurs to me," Eastcott said thoughtfully, "that if we wish to return to London today, I had best make sure my carriage is ready. Rogers was to have had it repaired and brought to Wixbridge by now. Come along, Lucinda! I perceive Tony and Miss Lyford wish to be alone."

"How astute of you!" Sir Anthony retorted good-naturedly.

Harry grinned, turned toward the door, then paused. "It also occurs to me, cousin, that you may wish to find more, er, suitable garments for Miss Lyford to wear."

With that bit of advice, Eastcott and his bride left, followed hastily by Richard Lyford. Oblivious to the presence of the landlord, Felicity told Sir Anthony, "Meg and George! I must find them. They have been so kind to me and . . . and my clothes are at their cottage."

Sir Anthony smiled down at his bride-to-be. "I, too, would like to see your friends again."

"Well I'm pleased to hear that," the innkeeper said, with awful sarcasm, "since, if you mean old Locke and his daughter, they've been waiting this quarter hour nor more to see *you!*"

"Then show them in," Woodhall replied shortly.

A few moments later Felicity found herself once more enveloped in Meg's embrace while Sir Anthony gripped George's hand. "Do we be wishing 'ee happy?" Meg asked with a grin.

"*Very* happy," Felicity confirmed.

"I don't doubt it!" Meg retorted, a twinkle in her eyes as she looked at Sir Anthony. "Do 'ee be getting married here or in Lunnon?"

"London," Woodhall replied gravely. "We return there today."

"'ee'll be wanting 'ees things," George observed.

"Could we go, now, to get them?" Felicity asked Sir Anthony. "And see Martha?"

"Lord love 'ee, no!" George protested, reddening. "Wouldn't be fittin'! Meg and me will fetch 'em. Aye, and Martha, too. She'll be wanting to take 'er leave of 'ee, I doubt me not."

Felicity hesitated, not sure of what to say. Sir Anthony, however, read the stern pride in George's eyes and answered quietly, "Thank you, you are very kind."

"'ee needn't fear we'll be long," Meg promised.

When they had left and the parlour door was once more shut, Sir Anthony gathered Felicity in his arms again. Her head nestled comfortably on his chest as she said, "I'd like to give Meg and Martha something. My earrings for Meg, perhaps, but I don't know what to give Martha."

"A bonnet?" Sir Anthony suggested.

"No, I—" Felicity broke off as she remembered something Martha had said. "I think I'd like to give her perfume. From France. She . . . she said she'd always wondered what it would be like to be a lady, all scented and such, and that it was the one thing she secretly covetted."

"We'll send some from London. Will that do?"

Felicity sighed. "You're very good to me."

"Baggage!" He responded affectionately and kissed her. Suddenly Sir Anthony laughed. "Can you imagine poor Tifton's face if we had returned to London with you looking like a country farm girl?"

Felicity grinned. "Perhaps you ought to abandon me somewhere along the way."

Sir Anthony looked down at her. "Oh, no!" he said

sternly. "I've finally got you and I shan't let you go! Not ever again."

Felicity nestled closer and said, in a provocative voice, "Unless, of course, I run away."

"If you ever so much as try, I shall . . . I shall. . . ."

"Yes?" Felicity turned her face up toward his and said hopefully, "What will you do?"

"This!" he retorted and swept her up in an embrace that threatened to crush Felicity.

She didn't mind in the least.

About the Author

April Lynn Kihlstrom was born in Buffalo, New York, and graduated from Cornell University with an M.S. in Operations Research. She, her husband, and their two children enjoy traveling and have lived in Paris, Honolulu, Georgia, and New Jersey. When not writing, April Lynn Kihlstrom enjoys needlework and devotes her time to handicapped children.